The County of Birches

STORIES

JUDITH KALMAN

St. Martin's Press ≈ New York

Some of these stories have appeared in slightly different form in the following publications: *The Fiddlehead, Saturday Night, Queen's Quarterly, Descant, Windsor Review, Grain, Prairie Fire,* and the 1997 *Journey Prize Anthology.* "Flight" was broadcast on CBC Radio's "Between the Covers."

ISBN 0-312-20886-3

First published in British Columbia by Douglas & McIntyre Ltd.

First U.S. Edition: September 1999

10   9   8   7   6   5   4   3   2   1

In memory of Gusztav Weinberger Kalman

ACKNOWLEDGEMENTS

This book would not have thrived without the care of the following individuals:

Murray Lamb, who read tirelessly through countless drafts and served as my agent, advisor, personal editor and chief support in every way; Anna Kalman Dollin, who let a lot go as literary licence and who provided inspiration; Elaine Kalman Naves, who shared unstintingly of her research on the Jewish middle class in northeastern Hungary, and who was my spiritual companion through the first crucial stages of the manuscript; Greta Hofmann Nemiroff, my ideal reader, who never let me forget I had to get back to writing; Marlene Kadar, who got me started by suggesting I might be an "immigrant writer" but earned a laugh of derision for her efforts; Nathan and Gideon, who returned to me the voices of childhood; Barbara Pulling, who accepted the manuscript and provided meticulous editorial guidance. To all of you, my heartfelt thanks.

I am also grateful to the Ontario Arts Council and the Canada Council for recognition and financial assistance.

CONTENTS

The
Old
World

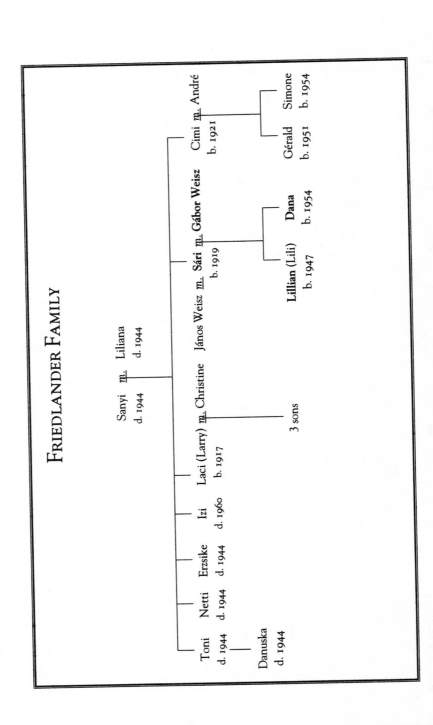

FRIEDLANDER FAMILY

Toni
d. 1944

Danuska
d. 1944

Netti
d. 1944

Erzsike
d. 1944

Izi
d. 1960

Laci (Larry) m. Christine
b. 1917

3 sons

Sanyi m. Liliana
d. 1944   d. 1944

János Weisz m. **Sári** m. Gábor Weisz
                b. 1919

Lillian (Lili)
b. 1947

Dana
b. 1954

Cimi m. André
b. 1921

Gérald
b. 1951

Simone
b. 1954

NOT

FOR ME

A CROWN

OF THORNS

"Come down," Sári hissed at her sister Cimi, glancing back at the white stuccoed house. Anyone stepping from the cook's entrance to the outhouse at the end of the verandah would notice the elm's trembling branches. Rózsa the cook, looking out the window over her broad, pine-planked counter, might glimpse a yellow hairbow winking through the elm's flame-shaped leaves. Pulling her hands from the bread dough, she'd descend on them in a trice, surprisingly agile despite her girth and shuffling slippers. More often than not she could spring from one side of the big kitchen to the other to smack away the fingers of one of the seven children—even the grown ones—anticipating the hand that would stealthily approach the cheesecloth covering her freshly baked *béles*.

When Sári and Cimi were little, Rózsa struck like lightning if they toddled into the path of the servant girl as she hauled a vat of steaming laundry off the wood-stoked stove. Little one screaming in the clutch of Rózsa's elbow and Rózsa shrieking too that now she had to do the work of the Fraulein! Poor mistress;

if she only knew the peril that stalked her brood. But better she was spared so she could preside in the shop with patience and grace. Rózsa liked to feel in charge. After all, it was she who had prepared the first solids to pass the lips of each of the babies, she who held the choicest morsels to their pink satin mouths, feeding them like birdlings from her hand. The Fraulein taught the babies to take food off a spoon, but it was Rózsa's privilege to give them the best bits from her thick red fingers.

"Get down *now!*" Sári commanded her sister, who had leapt into the tree without thinking.

Cimi ignored her. "Did you hear that? I'm sure I heard something. I know it's up there, poor little thing, and now it can't get back."

Before Sári could retort, "It's a cat. That's what cats do, they climb," Cimi had tucked her dress into her knickers and melted into the thick foliage of the elm's lowest boughs. They would be lucky if it was only Rózsa who caught them. Wiping her hands on her apron as she waddled across the lawn, she would instinctively reach up into the tree and haul Cimi back by the foot before she had gotten far. "Have you lost your senses?" she'd demand, giving Cimi a light cuff. "Don't you realize your Apuka will be home from the field at any moment?" But Cimi didn't realize anything when an impulse overcame her. If Sári had to go up after her, she'd give her plait a good yank.

"Just wait until Apuka gets hold of you," Sári threatened, but she found small comfort in the prospect because he would blame her too. Her father, losing his head in terror, would hold her responsible for letting Cimi climb. Sári chafed from the unfairness of it. *She* hadn't chased the cat up the tree.

At this very moment Apuka might be turning off the main road that led into town from the vineyards, his light coat draped over his shoulder, his head hatted like any good Jew, but not the flat round hat of the highly orthodox. His was contemporary and businesslike with a deep front V and a brim he pinched as he greeted an acquaintance. Apuka had little patience for the traditions of the devout. If they lost themselves in the scriptures and let their children starve, why shouldn't the world also believe it had a right to sweep them aside? As for the rich and holier-than-thou who scattered charitable disbursements in hopes of buying a seat in heaven, perhaps they believed the Lord's ear, too, might be purchased?

Apuka had no use for those who showed off their faith any more than he had for morning, afternoon and evening prayers. A blessing for the fruit of the earth, yes, naturally. As for rest, let the *yeshiva bochers* who came begging for their meals at the cook's entrance put in a few extra words for him. He wasn't ashamed to ask or to slip a coin into their pockets. He was a busy man. What else had *they* to do?

He gave a little snort, remembering the poor rabbinical student last week who had entered through the kitchen and been engulfed in the rich cooking odours that built up since daybreak. *Cholent* still baked in the great, wood-stoked oven, and a steaming soup steeped on the range. Rózsa ordered the boy to the table piled high with crockery, pointing a red arm bared by her rolled-up sleeve, so that the shamefaced student had to avert his eyes. While he squirmed uncomfortably, he heard voices raised in the other rooms, and then someone's skirts swished past him and out the door. Girls moved in and out to pick up clean washing and to tear chunks from the loaves that lined the counter. The bocher was afraid to raise his head lest he glimpse the pale flesh under an arm that reached up to fix a hairpin. By the time the servant girl had cleared him a place and pushed a bowl under his nose, he was too overwhelmed to eat.

"Nu—" Apuka's hard elbow had poked him in the back. "Does the Lord forbid even a bite of bread? Eat or you won't grow a beard long enough for the anti-Semites to tug."

While his daughters tittered, Apuka bent down to whisper, "No harm will take you here. *This* is not the devil's camp." And, as was his custom, pressed a few coins into the young man's fingers.

If Sári and Cimi were lucky, Apuka would be stalled a few moments along the way home by someone he knew. Well, business could always be better, but he daren't complain. As long as there was food on the table.

Food on the table and stores in the larder, chickens in the yard and fruit from his vines. Five beautiful daughters and two smart-mouthed sons, he mustn't seem ungrateful for the bounty of the Lord; nor dare he boast lest he tempt the evil eye. Apuka was shrewd and superstitious. Spitting into the dirt to ward off ill-intentioned hexes, he would tip his hat and continue home for his midday meal.

When he came in from the field, he was usually in good humour. If a child had a desire or appeal, now was the time to present it. Apuka was best approached while the outdoor air still filled his lungs, before he turned to town and the affairs of the shop. Rózsa would have cleared the sink of dishes for the master's arrival. Pumping the handle above the deep basin as Apuka rinsed what he called the "clean dirt" of the fields from his hands, the child would present his or her request. This was when Apuka felt most disposed to listen to the hankerings of his children: a few *filér* for the "useless cinema" the older ones frequented, or the porcelain-headed doll one of the girls had set her heart on. In the fall, after he'd been shut in at the shop for days on end, Apuka would lash out at the things he'd let his children accumulate, threatening to burn the dolls with the autumn leaves, "As if there aren't enough bodies underfoot already!" It would go especially hard for them, Sári thought, to disrupt Apuka's midday peace.

She looked up into the tree's twitching branches. Its thick foliage spread over her like a green sky dotted with stars of sunlight so sharp she had to squint. Cimi's legs drooped indolently above her. Anyone glancing from the house would notice the dangling legs without knowing exactly whose they were. After all, both little girls from that house ran around naked-legged in the sunshine save for the white ankle socks on their sandalled feet. It incensed her to be implicated in Cimi's caprice.

The cat wasn't hers. Like all cats, it had attached itself to Cimi. In the nursery last night, the kitten seemed hardly more than a balled-up sock, or a pom-pom that might hang on the tie of a fur-trimmed hood.

"Shut up," Cimi had warned her before she could protest the

presence of a cat in their bed and alert Fraulein to another flouting of the household's rules. "It's too little to have any fleas yet. Just look at it."

Sári ran a finger along the delicate spine of the kitten. Its grey fur was meltingly soft, like the downy head of a baby. It was impossibly sweet—but already Cimi's. It nestled only in the crook of Cimi's skinny arm. Cimi was a charmer of felines. She had but to breathe on a cat and it would let her do any-thing—wrap its head in a doll's bonnet or stuff it into a pram. They sheathed their claws for Cimi.

"Get down here, stupid," Sári ordered again, her throat sore from the strain of whispering.

"I heard it just this minute," Cimi called, not even trying to lower her voice. "I'll find it, even if you won't help."

"Idiot," Sári muttered. Sári would have to go up there to silence her before Apuka heard.

She put a sandal on the bark of the tree, feeling for the famil-iar knot she braced herself against when she mounted. They had all climbed that tree, each child in his or her time. But never under Apuka's nose. Like the others she was an able climber. Maybe not quite as sure-footed as Cimi, who could shimmy up effortlessly. But then neither was Sári such a stupid goat as to run headlong into resistance. There was no budging Apuka on the subject of trees, not even such a healthy and venerable one as this elm with so many branches you could climb it like a ladder. They had each of them tried at least once to persuade him.

"Apukám, it's such a safe tree—look at it," they pleaded. "All those sturdy branches so close together. You'd have to be crip-pled not to climb it."

"Bite your tongue," Apuka thundered, and his hand flew up as though to strike them but hovered, instead, above his own head. "You don't know what you're talking about. Your Mamuka's brother, he was a big shot, ya, a know-it-all like you. But he fell out of a tree. Just once!" At this point Apuka raised his other hand and joined the two in a hard smack. "And that was that."

"Goat—stupid, stubborn, willful," Sári seethed as she craned to see where Cimi had clambered.

Sári's mouth pursed grimly as she followed her sister. Once when they were little, Cimi had nearly disfigured her. It was just by chance that the brick she had thrown caught Sári on the hairline. The madness of Cimi, not more than four or five at the time, Apuka's old fedora flopping over her eyes. She tipped up the hat, revealing eyes that flared a blue fury. Levelling them in deadly aim at her bossy sister, she pronounced before firing, "This is one time too many you made me be the Father!"

Sári had stood transfixed by the flash storm that transformed her tender-hearted and usually obliging sister. Spellbound, she watched the brick lurch in her direction. Blood ran warmly down her face, spilling onto Mamuka's old gown that bespoke Sári's role as Mother. Only when Sári saw her own blood and realized, outraged, that she had been struck by her sister did she gasp with pain, wind slicing exposed flesh. They were just a year apart, raised like twins, the last of the litter. Both of them were shocked into silence by this rupture that oozed sticky and red between them. Not until Rózsa's arrival and then the Fraulein's did the predictable howls and commotion begin.

Sári touched the scar on her forehead before she reached for the branch overhead. Early on, her features had shown promise of her older sisters' mild beauty. She knew from their experience that a natural dowry would be useful when she grew up, fourth of five sisters. She quickly learned to value and exploit her appearance. Like Mamuka, who used the best fabrics from the shop to fashion their outfits. Even the boys were her mannequins. The children's charming features and Mamuka's handsome garments made the best advertisement for the wares of the shop. Six children lent themselves more or less willingly to this purpose. But then there was Cimi, mercurial and unthinking, who one Pesach, dressed in holiday velvet, refused to wait patiently on the front yard lawn while Mamuka buttoned the endless rows on the other children's frocks and jackets. Cimi had wandered away and ruined her vestments in the shitpile down the road.

Sári's legs pumped purposefully up the rungs of the elm. How often must she contend with the thoughtlessness of her sister? There was that other time too, Rózsa's gleaming gutting knife poised in Cimi's fingers: "There's going to be a funeral around here, Miss Schoolteacher *Sarah*," she'd spat because Sári had tried to crown her with a dunce cap.

This time Sári was going to stop Cimi in her tracks before, as the elder, she'd be made to pay the price.

"Where are you? I'm coming," she hissed up into the branches.

"Shh," Cimi answered from closer than Sári had expected. "Listen, I think I hear something." She had straddled a limb above Sári on the other side of the trunk.

"I don't care," Sári said, joining her, "we can get it later. We may still have time to get down before Apuka sees."

"What? Do you think he'll climb up to get us? Besides, he doesn't have to notice. We'll go down after he leaves."

"Don't be stupid," Sári snapped. "We can't stay up here forever. You better come down now before you get any more bright ideas."

"You think you know everything, don't you?" Cimi flicked a braid over her shoulder, catching Sári on the cheek. "Shut up. I'm sure I heard it, poor little pet."

Cimi pulled herself to her feet. Balancing her fingers against the trunk, she slid along the branch until she got a clearer view. Then she stretched her other arm into the leaves overhead. The branch dipped from the weight of her movements, and Sári had a brief sensation of vertigo as she watched Cimi grope blindly at the ungraspable air.

"Watch it," she admonished, forgetting not to care. "It's only a cat." The plaintive mewing of the kitten could be heard faintly through the rustling leaves. Well, that sealed it. The creature wasn't *only* a cat to Cimi; if it breathed, it was blessed. There would be no getting Cimi down until the cat was in hand.

Cimi let go the trunk and sidled further along the limb, making soothing noises to the kitten. Sári fumed. What if Cimi the fool slipped? Cimi had no right to upset her by being so reckless and sure of herself. She was always selfish, not once considering how Sári might feel stuck up here, unable to do anything but watch and worry. *She* wasn't such an idiot as to startle Cimi now, or get her into an argument. *She* wasn't one to imperil her sister.

"There!" Cimi leapt up like a gymnast, and now swung from the overhanging branch.

"Stop it! Right now!" Sári shouted, unable to keep from raising her voice. "Now! Do you hear me, Cimi? You get back here now!"

Cimi's legs swayed above the limb she had balanced on, and she inched her palms towards the thinning edge of the branch overhead. Then, in a swift move that forced Sári's heart into her mouth, Cimi let go her right hand and grabbed at thin air. Sári saw something grey explode from the leaves while Cimi's legs scissored.

"Idiot!" she yelled, but Cimi had already swung back to the trunk and dropped like a cat herself to the limb below. Around her neck the kitten clung like a fur collar.

"Down! Both of you! Get down here!" Their father's voice cracked through the golden noon light. He choked out the order. From the girls' perch they saw his fist raised against them, and behind it his upturned twisted face.

Apuka's passions played through his body as through an instrument. He had a quick, impatient mind that expressed itself in neuralgic aches and pains, headaches, a delicate stomach. His terror of heights translated into rage.

"Get down. Brats. Disobedient wretches. Get what you deserve!"

The tree shook and shuddered around Sári, alive with a swift wind. Cimi, kitten clutching her shoulder, had taken flight and was climbing again, impossibly higher.

"Cimi! Sárika!" a chorus called from the foot of the tree. Rózsa, red-faced and wringing her hands in her apron. Háni the servant girl, gazing up blankly until Rózsa slapped her awake to send her running, Sári presumed, to fetch Mamuka from the shop. Looking down from her roost she noticed that her quick-tongued brother Laci was chewing ruminatively on lunch, hands in the pockets of his short pants. Fraulein appeared finally, calling their names as though she had been searching for them this long while. She'd feel a guilty twinge or two before this was over, Sári relished. Toni, their eldest sister, graceful as a willow, leaned gently towards the elm, hand shielding her eyes from the glare. Cimi shouted at them all from aloft: "You can't make me!"

And now Sári too joined the fracas. "Stupid. Don't be so stupid. It's just a spanking!"

She strained her eyes up into the shaking branches where, instead of finding Cimi, she was struck by the rays of the sun. White and blinding they pierced through the leaves, obliterating her sister. When she glanced down again at the gathering of her kin they were sprayed by sun spots that left brilliant holes in their chests, bellies and eyes. She was stunned by the blasted peace of the noontime idyll. The green and gold canopy that had sheltered two little girls and a baby kitten, the dangling of skinned knees and sagging socks and sandals the colour of milk chocolate shattered like a picture in glass.

Alone in the tree, Sári felt stripped suddenly of all that rooted her. A weightlessness filled her head. The earth moved ever so slightly as though she might lift off and spin like a balloon on a current of air. She could pass out of this world now, lift, and let go.

"Sar-i-ka!" Rózsa's scream pierced Sári's reverie, making her grab involuntarily at the tree trunk. "You'll be sorry, Miss," shouted the cook, "if I have to come up there to get you!"

How had she gotten into this, Sári wondered, dazed by the fear of those below and the dangerous flight overhead of her sister. She was a good girl. She hadn't gone looking for trouble. Her head felt light and her eyesight spotty. What she had witnessed seared through her like a brand. What was it? Something so troubling it made her float free of her body as though she were lighter than air. She didn't like the sensation. It was too dangerous and too eerie and she had no patience for what she couldn't understand.

"Do you hear me, Miss? I can climb if I have to!"

Sári didn't recognize herself in what she had experienced. It made her chilly to think she had almost lost her grounding.

"Nitwits," Laci laughed up at them, "are you going to climb up to the sun?"

Well, Cimi might think she could escape forever, but Sári wanted none of it. Slowly and carefully, she placed one foot below the other. She descended with relief, regretting only the decline of her role in the drama.

Too stiff with panic to cast about for a switch or loosen his belt, Apuka beat her with his bare hand. Face smeared with tears and snot, head upside down because she was bent over, Sári barely made out the grey blur that streaked into the grass a moment before Apuka pushed her away so he could spring after her sister. Feckless, sly Cimi had waited until Apuka was absorbed in the beating, then scrambled down the tree trunk and sprinted off.

"Cimi, get back here!"

But Cimi ran and ran, her legs toughened by climbing trees and dodging the boys from the Christian Fathers' lycée, who tried to pull her braids and worse if they could catch her. Apuka staggered home puffing, his shirt soaked with sweat, hand on his heaving chest. Mamuka waited in the sitting room. Deploring the spectacle her daughters had made of themselves, she sat stitching, her mouth an eloquent line.

Sári barely noticed the shadows lengthen along the nursery floorboards. All afternoon she lay on the bed, face stuffed into her pillow. Her parents' voices, low and conciliatory, wafted from the main room where Mamuka had spread her sewing on the divan that pulled out nightly for the older girls' bed. Tonight there would be no guests invited to sip cordials and enjoy the big girls' renditions of operetta numbers. The young ones, lying two by two in the nursery, wouldn't keep each other awake with scary stories about the one-legged beggar who prowled the streets of the Jewish quarter. There would be no pauses to listen to laughter ripple from the adjacent room when their sisters finished a popular song, and no succumbing to giggles that made the Austrian Fraulein get up time and again muttering her guttural hushes. The household was still in the aftermath of its midday crisis. It was quiet with implied recriminations and apologies.

Sári heard the subdued sounds of the household from a spiritual remove. They had abandoned her and left her to her misery. Nobody cared. When Apuka came back sweating and panting, he had tried to take her in his arms.

"It's all over now, Sárika darling. You're home and safe."

But she had shaken free. Over for him, perhaps, now that he didn't need to worry. But what about her? No one seemed to care about what she felt.

"Really, Sanyi." Mamuka's grey eyes had widened when she saw how dishevelled Apuka looked. Sufficiently quelled, he went straight to the pump and scooped water over his neck. Sári, sticky and sopping, waited in the door for attention. She had been frightened too, and then beaten and humiliated. But Mamuka only swiped at Sári's face distractedly with her lace handkerchief and sat her down at the table with a glass of water. Sári stared into the glass, tears welling. It wasn't fair. She had been dutiful. She'd only gone up into the tree to fetch Cimi down. She hadn't run away and given Apuka a pain in his side. No one felt the slightest bit sorry for the wrong Sári had suffered. Her tears fell into the glass, and turned to sobs.

"Sárika," Mamuka sighed. "You know you gave your father such a fright."

Fright! Her fright had been worse. She'd been subjected to Cimi's acrobatics in the air. She had swayed in the tree and nearly lost her balance. What if Apuka had seen that! His fright was nothing compared to hers, but no one took her feelings into account. Sári put her hand on her heart and sobbed even harder.

"What's this," Laci teased, "is someone still beating you?"

Such an insult, to have her suffering made light of.

In the end there was nothing for it but to let Rózsa lift Sári in her big arms and carry her, legs trailing limply, to bed in the nursery.

She conjured sorrowful scenarios that stoked her tears. How sorry they all would be when she died of her broken heart, her brief, tender life sacrificed by an unfeeling family. Then they would be exposed for their heartlessness. Cimi would be banished for the trouble she had made. She would get her reward finally for all the wrongs she had inflicted on her blameless sister. They would cast Cimi out of the family fold. When no one was looking, after the funeral cortege had finished its bitter business of burying Sári's young, beautiful body, Cimi would crawl out from among the cemetery willows like a cast-out cur, and throw herself weeping on Sári's grave.

The sad and gratifying image sustained Sári through the long afternoon.

Too restless to coop himself up at the shop after an unnaturally quiet midday meal, Apuka drifted out onto the back lawn. He gazed quizzically at the huge elm. It had been here long before he had brought his bride to the house not even a decade into the century, more than twenty years ago. The house had appealed to him because of its proximity to the road that led from Beregszász's Jewish quarter to the vineyards and groves of the surrounding countryside. In the days of his father, the land had been Russian. Sometimes Russian, sometimes Magyar or Austro-Hungarian. In any case they had remained Jews, whoever was master. Like the tree, they were rooted here and fixed in place.

Tentatively Apuka touched the bark. It was just a tree, beautiful, shapely, a green fact he normally took satisfaction from when he left the house at dawn through the kitchen entrance. He'd glance at the tree dominating his yard, and think yes, it was anchored here. Whatever ill wind might blow through, it would hold firm.

Today the hand of fate had brushed, wrongways, up the hair on his nape. A buyer had come out to the field that morning. As a rule, Apuka preferred to conduct business in the more formal setting of his shop, but occasionally a prospective client wished to make an inspection before placing his order. Those who dealt with Apuka year after year—the local Jewish merchants and distillers—trusted the quality of his fruit, but sometimes buyers came from farther afield when the crop had failed in a neighbouring county. It was natural for them to wish to look over the vineyard.

Apuka watched, at ease in the doorway of his rough office, really a shack, as the stranger alighted from his sputtering motor car. The weather had obliged Apuka this season. His yield was nothing to be ashamed of. The fieldhands looked up too at the sound of the motor. Hereabouts farmers and businessmen alike got around mainly on foot or by horse and buggy. The buyer was a stocky fellow who wore the waist-cinched suit with breeches of a country gentleman, not the flowing coat of a town Jew.

"Herr Friedlander," he extended his thick hand briskly towards Apuka. Odd that the stranger used the German rather than Hungarian Úr. Perhaps he had Austrian connections, thought Apuka.

"You, Herr, have something I believe I require," the customer pronounced ostentatiously.

Although he was put off somewhat by the fellow's manner, Apuka wouldn't let it stand in the way of making a sale. He drew the stranger out towards the upper field that was yet to be harvested. The man's Hungarian wasn't tinged with an accent, Apuka noted after asking him where he had driven from that day. The German usage was obviously a pretension. Well, it wasn't too much to ask of himself to overlook an irritating mannerism in the interest of making a profitable deal. Apuka pointed out the dense clusters of grapes on the sun-thinned vines, inviting the client to taste each variety.

"But Herr Friedlander," the buyer interrupted with what struck Apuka as an inappropriate laugh, "I have come to make a sale myself. In effect, to sell my own person."

"Sir?" Apuka pulled back coolly despite his reminder to himself to give the customer the benefit of the doubt.

"I have a modest but prospering homestead near Munkács. In fact, we are mutually connected through your cousin Frau

Blanka Gyorgy, whom your charming daughter Antonia visited this spring. There we enjoyed a brief, but I am flattered to believe, profound understanding." At this he stopped and looked at Apuka so pointedly the hairs rose on the back of Apuka's neck. "In short, I'm convinced we would make a successful match."

This odious man was claiming a personal relationship to him and his *daughter*. Apuka's head felt wet beneath his hatband. Who did this stranger think he was to come out here in his motor car and field boots, flaunting German affectations and claims to Toni's affections. What kind of a Jew would ask for a hand in marriage without, at least, a formal introduction? Indeed, what species of Jew was he? Apuka imagined himself to be a forward-thinking businessman, but certain proprieties were unassailable. No wonder this man rubbed him the wrong way with his beardless brazen face and clipped head naked beneath the blue eye of God's ether.

"Sir," Apuka barely contained his agitation. He tipped back his hat as if to accommodate the blood that rushed to his head. "I don't know you, your family, nor even which *rebbe* you follow."

"Rebbe?" The word plopped from the stranger's mouth, like a pebble ingested by mistake. "Jew? Herr Friedlandler," the suitor bridled in turn, "you take me for a *Jew*!"

Apuka felt lightheaded. How could he have been so blind not to realize the stranger wasn't Jewish? He was a *goy*, not here to buy fruit from a Jewish grower, but to *take* something far more valuable. A goy, shaved and hatless, and—in all likelihood—with foreskin intact. *Asking for his daughter.* Had the natural order of things suddenly become skewed?

"How dare you," choked Apuka, and managed again only, "how could you dare presume ...?"

"Me?" demanded the goy with insufferable arrogance. "You should be grateful for the chance of marrying her out of this mire!"

Apuka sent the stranger packing so fast he didn't even learn his name. Although epithets were exchanged, he congratulated himself on maintaining the presence of mind to keep his hands off the fellow.

It unnerved him, that he was so much in the dark he didn't know what his children were up to. Had Toni been hiding, all these months, a secret correspondence? How could he be expected to protect them and help them make the right choices for their lives if they kept from him the most important details?

When Apuka had first brought his bride to the white-washed, single-storey structure that would be their home, the elm seemed to welcome them with its outstretched beckoning boughs. Inwardly, he saluted it like the sturdy sentinel it brought to mind. At that time the house consisted of two commodious chambers, the kitchen and the main room that served for everything else. They had entered through the main room's portal at the front of the house and surveyed its generous proportions. These days the door was permanently blocked by the walnut chiffonier that held drawers of table linens. And the two rooms had grown to four. The family had burgeoned, requiring first a nursery addition, then spilling into the main room and raising the need for a chamber for the parents. The rooms opened one into the other. Nights, after the lights were extinguished in the main room, Mamuka and Apuka passed through the nursery that breathed with the syncopated rhythms of their babies, to their own room that was small but luxurious in its privacy. The newel-posted bed was weighted by silk eiderdowns and goose-feathered pillows in monogrammed slipcovers. Now Apuka marvelled at how quickly their children had sprung into the world. The bed had spawned five girls and two boys in hardly a dozen years. Each child had added exponentially to his cares.

Apuka had heard Sári yelling before he turned into the yard. Liliana was always chiding the children not to shout like peasants, but you couldn't monitor them each moment. He looked across the lawn to see what the little girls were doing. That's when he spotted them hanging out on the edge of the limb as thoughtlessly as birds.

Apuka looked up into the tree again. It had failed him, or at least misled him. Its permanence didn't seem at all reassuring.

There was treachery in its massive, unwieldy bulk. The thing was trapped by its roots, ingrown as much as it was growing. And it could snatch from him what was most precious with its high ensnaring fingers.

Shadows collected on the lawn, but Apuka still felt the heat of the summer sun in the warm bark. It passed into his palm. They were rooted here, he and the elm. But what about his children? When he pictured them up in the high branches of the tree, he panicked. He saw them, light-boned and delicate, singing their modern songs guilelessly. What if an ill wind were to blow through? A wind dark and fierce with malice, that blew them away to the ends of the earth? He felt unsure of himself and sensitive to his shortcomings, especially following Liliana's disapproval of his outburst. Perhaps she would think he had been reckless too chasing that anti-Semite off their land.

Cimi lounged along a thick bough overhead, looking down at her father. He seemed too subdued. The odd way he touched the tree made her uncomfortable. Apuka wasn't given to moody reflection. He was active and opinionated and as likely to burst into song as one of his children. What was he doing communing with a tree trunk? She wanted to distract him. Poor Apuka, to be so troubled over a big old tree that was as solid and safe as the ground.

She was up again in the offending tree, so she hesitated from calling down right away, even though Apuka looked in need of comfort. She was more accustomed to his flash rages. All she had to do was lead him on a chase; eventually he tired of his anger. Today she had circled back to the yard after shaking Apuka off her scent, then taken refuge for the afternoon in the very place no one would expect her to have the audacity to hide. For the first time Cimi regretted provoking her father. She must have upset him a great deal, she thought, to cause him to hang about like this. Poor Apuka to be so needlessly worked up. She and her siblings were as sure-footed as mountain goats. The tree was like a second home. She had lain on the branch all afternoon, idly breaking off twigs and leaves, and working them in her fingers until she found she could twine them together. As she fashioned the sticks and flakes of bark into something that had shape, she forgot all about the time despite the gnawing in her stomach. When Apuka came outside, she was just beginning to notice that the sun's rays had faded.

"Apuka," she risked calling as he turned away. "Apuka, wait!"

The sound of Cimi's voice pulled Apuka's heartstrings. Fool, he was as sentimental as he was hot-tempered. Soon he would get teary-eyed like his daughters over a popular ballad. Cimi scrambled down the trunk and he felt a rush of gratitude as though the tree had relented and returned, unharmed, his youngest, wildest bird. Let this be a lesson then to stop brooding and count his blessings.

"There you are, you naughty child. You better come in and have a word with your sister."

Cimi was sorry about Sári's spanking, but it was Sári's own fault that she hadn't tried to get away. She was always telling Cimi what to do as though she knew everything, but look what it had gotten her. Cimi knew Sári would blame her, and Sári could be unforgiving. Cimi nestled contentedly in Apuka's arms. Well, it wouldn't hurt to beg Sári's pardon. Cimi, after all, had escaped.

"What have you got there?" asked Apuka, noticing the circlet in her hand.

"See," she said playfully, "I've made you a crown."

He laughed proudly, observing the clever way she had worked the rough, hard wood of the elm. His children weren't just beautiful. They were clever and talented, blessed with the gifts of the Lord.

"That will never get around my thick skull." Apuka patted Cimi dotingly, forgetting for once to deceive the evil eye by pretending to spit on her creation. "You'll just have to wear it yourself."

Sári stirred from her pool of misery when she heard them come in. The creak of the kitchen door plucked her attention. It was about time Cimi made an appearance and got what she deserved.

"So," pronounced Rózsa weightily, "the prodigal comes back."
An uncertain silence hung in the air for a moment.

"On Apuka's shoulders? More like the conquering hero."
Laci's saucy rejoinder broke the tension. Led by Mamuka's barely
suppressed chortle, the family burst out laughing.

To Sári, sequestered with her burden of mistreatment, their
good humour felt like a slap. How could they *laugh*? A joke was
all it took for them to overlook Cimi's offence?

"Yes!" Cimi chirped, quick to capitalize on the good mood,
"I even have a laurel wreath like Caesar!"

Sári froze. Now Cimi evidently was showing off something
the others greeted with delight. Sári hated what Cimi had
made, even before she laid eyes on it. With just some trinket,
Cimi had dispelled the afternoon's solemnity in a second. Was
that how cheaply justice could be bought? Sári felt violated.
Cimi had hurt her *again*, but everyone ignored it. Outrage
staunched her tears and withered her self-pity. She felt walled
off from her family by her sense of injury. Sári was the good
child. That should count for something!

She remembered the bible story she had puzzled over more
than once since the first time she heard it, the story about Noah
and the flood. Sári sympathized with the Lord's desire to wash
away evil. She readily accepted the premise that the world had
gone bad and just one man alone remained true to the laws of
the Lord. One good man and his family remained among a world
of God-deniers and sinners, and they deserved to be rewarded.
She even accepted that the Lord would spare only two of each
kind; after all, the other species were just animals. She imagined the ark rocking forty days and forty nights under a black
sky—the lightless, endless days. They must have become very
attached to each other, man and beast alike. The last ones left
on the face of the earth.

What Sári couldn't understand was why Noah *twice* released
birds to see if the waters had receded. The second bird was a
dove. What about the first? A nameless bird released too soon,
it flew high and wide but didn't return. That didn't seem fair.
The bird was just doing what it was told. A premature courier,

it was defeated by the flood and dark clouds and not a dry twig in sight. Of all the Lord's punishments, this one seemed to Sári altogether heartless and wasteful. A blameless bird sent out at the Lord's command, and what for? Was He not all-knowing? He was fully aware that the floods had not subsided.

The nursery door opened quietly, light flooding the doorway. Cimi's slight figure swam in it. Some hero, Sári scoffed—skinny, small-boned, and wearing on her head an ugly, twiggy thing, no doubt the work of "art" Cimi had used to charm their family. Sári was disgusted with them for being so easily duped.

"What do you want?" Sári demanded. Cimi didn't approach right away, but floated in the portal. When she stepped into the room's darkness, it looked from Sári's position in bed that Cimi's feet sank through the light. It was nauseating. Cimi was rewarded for misbehaving while Sári had been made to suffer. She was sick from the injustice of it. And now Cimi had the nerve to look pathetic. Twigs and bark and spiky leaves stuck out from her hair. Did she expect Sári to feel sorry for *her*?

"Get lost," Sári threatened. "Leave me alone."

"Sári," Cimi said so meekly it made her sister uncomfortable, "don't hold it against me that I ran away. What would be the sense of both of us getting thrashed?"

She took off her crown and held it out as a peace offering. "Here. You can have it. I worked on it all afternoon."

Sári felt hard. She didn't know why she couldn't accept Cimi's apology. But her heart was hard and set. She felt unyielding and sure. She would never accept cheap reparation. She would have nothing to do with that wreath her sister had made. Her skin crawled to think of it prickly and poking on her head. She had been beaten and wronged, but not for her the crown of a martyr.

"Keep the stupid thing," Sári said, pushing it away, but Cimi looked crestfallen, so Sári relented grudgingly and made room for her sister in their bed.

"Listen," Cimi whispered after a bit. Sári heard nothing at first but the usual sounds of the household restored to its evening liveliness.

"Ssh," Cimi whispered again, "listen outside."

Sári tried to block out the black whistle by concentrating on nearer sounds. There was her father's gruff voice, followed by peals of girlish laughter. Apparently nobody in the main room heard anything out of the norm. Why, Sári pondered bitterly, must she?

Years later, Sári concluded that there was something wrong with the bible story because it offered no explanation for the punishment of the blameless. She would not go so far as to say that she found the *Lord* wanting, but His scribe had failed to adequately justify His actions.

In Auschwitz Cimi disappeared into herself, leaving behind her body. For a while, four of them were left: Sári and Cimi, Toni, and a cousin called Margit. The others had vanished. Apuka and his sons-in-law were dragged off with the men. Against Apuka's voluble insistence, Laci and their older brother Izi had refused to have anything to do with the vineyard and the shop. They had gone abroad to universities before the worst was upon them. But Mamuka and the sisters with the babies were taken from the main block and never seen again. In a last moment's inspiration, Mamuka had snatched the baby from the daughter standing nearest her, shouting, "Give me back my child." Fiercely hugging the screaming infant, Mamuka had pushed a stunned Toni towards Sárika. "Get away from my baby!"

Sári had pulled Toni in beside her and held on to her wrist. "Shut up," she hissed at her older sister, tugging her off before she snapped to. Sári didn't look back at Mamuka, or Netti, or Erzsike, or the babies she had helped to raise. She pulled Toni away in a vicelike grip.

You can't make someone live, though, Sári thought. You can give birth and feed and nurture, but you can't give life. Both Sári and Cimi had seen the same thing. All of them in the camp, running like ants under the hail of bullets pouring from a warplane. Sári ran, not knowing how she dodged, tripping over the fallen, or where she'd find cover. Stumbling over someone who moved, miraculously still stirred, although a hole, wide and open, gaped in the small of her back. Her cousin Margit. Sári caught the profile of the face already half ground into dirt. And as she blundered beneath the hail, she saw others too with holes riddled through them. Cimi flashed across the yard, then both of them were riveted by a figure upright and gently swaying, the only ant not scurrying but inclined towards the hail. When it shattered over them again, Sári and Cimi were sent flying. But Toni accepted the bullets like an ascent. She didn't fall, but rose to meet them.

Since then, it was harder to keep Cimi going. Ordered to file in, Sári would pull Cimi along. In the queue for food, she poked Cimi to remind her to hold out her tin plate. It occurred to Sári that, squatting over the shitpile, Cimi might actually let her muscles give way and sink into the filth. They would be ordered to bury her in it were such an accident to occur. But Sári knew it would be no mistake. Cimi's withdrawal was as steady as the shuffling advance of the queue that snaked towards the showers. Eventually Sári found herself thinking more about Cimi than herself. She was almost grateful to her for it.

Leaning against the wooden shell of the barracks, Cimi's jaw slackened. She could sit immobile and in such complete absence from her body, the spit would collect at the corner of her mouth. When no one was looking, Sári stroked Cimi's cheek to make its reflex tighten up. But she couldn't work Cimi's muscles forever.

"Idiot!" the *kapo* shouted, belting Cimi's loose mouth. "Do you know what happens to idiots in this place?"

The hatred of the Jewish overseer assigned to their block wasn't specific. He satisfied himself with kicking any of them in the ribs to make them get up. But the weakest among them especially enflamed his fury; a bruise was an invitation for him to beat it again.

Cimi didn't flinch. Perhaps she had already abandoned her nerves. Infuriated, the kapo pawed her eyelid, prying it up. "Do you think you can make me believe you're sick?"

He shoved his thumb into her eyeball and pressed, grinding

his thumb into the socket until Sári feared the eye might ooze out like the white of an egg. Not a muscle twitched in Cimi's face. But her arm rose like a crank. It came up effortlessly, trained in a trajectory that hit the kapo in the face. She had been absent ever since they lost Toni, but she returned to hit the kapo. Hit him with the hard back of her hand. A *reflex?* The kind of reflex that made you kick a mad dog that was foaming at the mouth. A reflex that made you climb to the treetop where its branches had thinned to matchsticks. A reflex of defiance, or a penchant for death?

A picture of Rózsa the cook appeared to Sári, Rózsa as she had been when Sári and Cimi were little girls, not wasted like the last time Sári had seen her, before Rózsa and all the others were taken to be gassed. Rózsa as she had stood under the elm like a tree herself, an extension of the earth that fed and formed them, Rózsa ordering Sári down from where she had drifted high above the elm: "You'll be sorry, Miss, if I have to come up there to get you!" Sári had chosen terra firma, but Cimi had continued climbing, higher and higher.

The kapo's blows broke the thin skin on Cimi's skull. Blood poured from her split head and smashed nose and raw cheek. Paralyzed with horror, Sári felt captive to the love that forced her to witness. Helpless, mute, numbness instantly filling the cavity as it was torn open inside her, she watched. Inured against the onset of anguish, Sári drifted to a plane where she was totally alone.

A rifle butt cracked on concrete, so close Sári's heart might have stopped if it weren't already suspended. "Enough!" a voice commanded in a German supercilious with disgust. Sári slid to the ground, joining her sister who had started to scream.

She stuffed her rag of a skirt into Cimi's mouth to stifle the cries that welled from the place where she'd been hiding. For evidently Cimi had been in hiding. Hiding somewhere in a secret place. Not that far away, but very carefully hidden. Sári resented her for it, even as she held down her raving sister. Somehow Cimi had managed, for a time, to escape. Sári stopped Cimi's mouth with her filthy skirt. She held her sister down as

Cimi writhed and bucked in her blood. The bird who couldn't bring herself to return with the terrible news of what she had seen. Sári rejected the vision as she sensed she had before in that other life she mustn't remember so clearly. Despite the evidence of Sári's eyes and ears and heart's blind crashing, they were not dumb animals, blameless and expendable. Sári still believed that she counted.

GRÓSZMANN CSALÁD

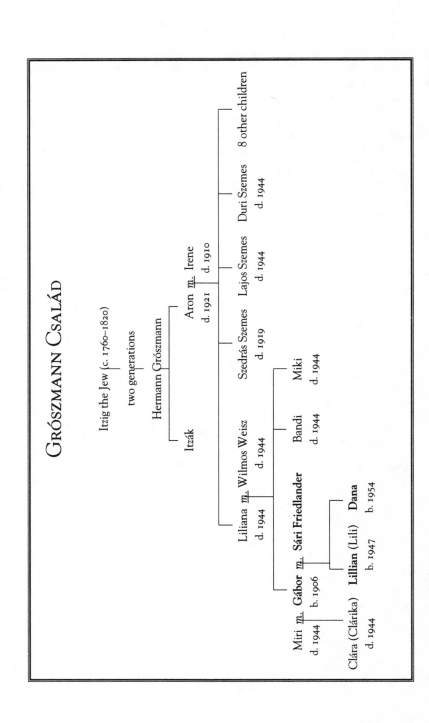

Itzig the Jew (c. 1760–1820)

two generations

Hermann Grószmann

Itzák

Aron m. Irene
d. 1921   d. 1910

Szedrás Szemes   Lajos Szemes   Duri Szemes   8 other children
d. 1919   d. 1944   d. 1944

Liliana m. Wilmos Weisz
d. 1944

Bandi   Miki
d. 1944   d. 1944

Miri m. Gábor m. Sári Friedlander
d. 1944   b. 1906

Clára (Clárika)   Lillian (Lili)   Dana
d. 1944   b. 1947   b. 1954

What's

in a

Name?

My father Gábor's life was split down the middle. Before the Fall was Life; then came the Word. Gábor's mouth filled with verbs parsed in past tense, and Life was rendered in telling.

The story began every November. "The surrounding countryside was poor and sandy," said Gábor, "but the Rákóczi Tanya bloomed like an oasis in the desert. In a manner of speaking, we came to life between the Tigris and Euphrates Rivers. We lived on the Lord's riches and with His blessing like the first man and woman in their Garden of Joy. And for a time we multiplied."

"We," I didn't have to be reminded, was Gábor's sweeping reference to the Grószmann *család*, some of whom had given up the name Grószmann, following the lead of Gábor's Uncle Szedrás and opting to Magyarize their name during the Great War. The more tradition-loving, pious members of the family persisted by way of Grószmann, but their kin, beloved notwithstanding because this family—*család*—solved their differences by inclusion, changed their name to Szemes, meaning clearsighted and clever—or corn fodder—depending on its usage. Gábor used it both ways, the former as it represented the family's progressive, worldly character before the Fall, and the latter referring to their outcome, especially during his seasonal bout of melancholy.

This name-playing, Gábor noted with more pride than irony, went on in a family that before it became a család was without a name altogether, descended from one Itzig the Jew who had surfaced on the sandy plain of northeastern Hungary not much more than a century earlier. Itzig the Jew, a wanderer (it would not have occurred to Gábor to contemplate an ancestor as a wastrel), too spent to drift any further, settled for and on the sand-blown turf of an obscure nation steeped in feudal tradition. In Itzig's time, as for centuries, Hungarian society was divided between the rich and the wretchedly poor. This orphaned or wander-lusting Jew, blown here like an errant seed from another barren dirt-poor corner of central Europe, became the progenitor of what Gábor described as an anomalous bourgeois, name-shuffling, gold-disbursing család-clan.

Here Gábor might interject that he had tried name-playing too, after the Fall, but had lacked the flair for it. His father, "your dearly beloved grandfather Wilmos Weisz," he would instruct as though I might forget my grandfather's name one year to the next, had made his home among his in-laws the Gröszmanns, as a partner to Gábor's Grandfather Aron. After the Second World War when the great estates were dismantled and the land owners disenfranchised, Gábor wasn't deeply affronted. It was, by then, a redundant expropriation. But his father's name was precious and he was loathe to give it up. Weisz was both Germanic and Jewish, and the Soviets bore no love for either. Dogged, true, lacking imagination for anything but what he remembered, Gábor substituted, for the necessary interval, his father's given name for his surname.

This abysmal lack of vision for the possibilities of make-over I imagine would have caused Uncle Szedrás Szemes to baptize Gábor in spittle for the second time in Gábor's life. "I came into this world blue and disfigured with the umbilicus strangling my breath," Gábor intoned, "so ugly that my Uncle

Szedrás spontaneously baptized me. Presented with his sister's first-born, the first of his beloved father's grandchildren, Uncle Szedrás reared in disgust. 'You call this a baby! I call it—phph!' And he christened me with saliva."

Swaggering, military-blue-breasted Uncle Szedrás was the one who had coined the Magyar name Szemes before joining the select Kaiser Wilhelm Hussars. Ostensibly it was to deflect military attention from his Jewishness, but some family members argued that perhaps Szedrás had wished to overlook his Jewishness himself. He, a descendent of Itzig the Nothing, had joined company with the mediaeval Counts Zichy and Esterház to pledge life and honour for Franz Josef. And his dull nephew, Gábor remarked with self-deprecating humour, grew up to lack the ingenuity to leave the past behind. I assumed my great-uncle Szedrás would have drawn a mouthful of contempt and aimed it again, with precision, between Gábor's eyes.

Szedrás rocked impatiently on the heels of his knee-high field boots, glancing every few moments out the front room window to see if the children had mounted.

"Patience, *édes ocsém*," the children's mother counselled, calming her voice to the register she used with this brother. She was older than Szedrás and entitled to call him "darling little brother," but he was the first son, heady with self-importance. He tolerated the diminutive because she was regarded by everyone for her exalted faith. In their often intemperate and populous household, Liliana was the soft-spoken but ruling chatelaine.

"Three *pischers*, what do they have so much to talk about? This isn't the Congress of Berlin," Szedrás fretted.

If Liliana showed any distress, it was through silence. Szedrás's present to her sons pained her. It was ostentatious, and excessive, reminding her of the Magyar gentry. She recoiled at the thought of her sons fawning over the *goyishe* plaything. Typical of Szedrás, dearly as she loved him, he had not asked her leave first, nor her husband's. At least he should have warned *his* father what manner of rig he was introducing to Aron's grandsons. But Liliana knew that her father would no more have forbidden Szedrás this gesture than she herself could deprive her boys of their delight in the toy.

The two older boys were engaged in negotiations over who would drive the ponies. Little Miki, knowing that as youngest his turn would come last, had mounted into the carriage and was admiring its beautiful red leather seat. It was the colour of the boots of the little peasant girls who danced in national dress on the Feast of St. Stephen. He snuffled the warm new leather smell.

"Hey," interrupted Bandi, "don't go rubbing your snot on it. If you're going to act like a baby, we're not taking you."

Miki bit his lip indignantly.

Gábor interceded, tightening his hold on the reins. "The gift is for us *all*," he reminded Bandi. Gabi was tiring, and he listed more obviously when he tired. He could feel his military uncle's eyes boring through the window's glass. It was humiliating enough to have to wear a corset like a woman, but he didn't want to shame himself in front of Szedrás-*bácsi* by relinquishing the reins to his younger brother.

"Look, I'll show you how to get up to the box without letting go," Bandi said, reaching for the lead.

Gabi would have to settle the matter so he could sit down and take the weight off his back.

"I'm quite capable, thank you. I know very well how the coachman mounts his box." Before his illness Gabi had been as lavishly praised as the other children among their kin. His sense of worthiness hadn't much corroded. After all, Anyuka assured him that he would recover and be well enough to ride as gallantly as Uncle Szedrás; it didn't so much matter that his aunts and uncles held their tongues.

"Let's go," Miki needled, bored with waiting.

Ignoring him, Bandi pressed his claim. "Gabi, you're holding the reins much too tight. You'll choke them if you try climbing up like that," he said, exasperated.

In the house Szedrás pawed the floor, more impatient than the ponies who decorously stood their ground.

"That's your boys for you, darling sister," he fumed, as close as he would get to criticizing her. There was nothing sarcastic in his address; in his estimation she *was* édes. But less so her sons, all jawing and no action. What should boys do with a coach and pair, but jump in and drive off? What was there to discuss about it?

According to Gábor, "On that day at the beginning of the First World War, Szedrás-bácsi had breakfasted in agitation. Every few moments he stood up to look out the window as though he were expecting someone. 'Surely, öcsém,' Anyuka questioned, 'you cannot be awaiting more special news?' For just recently Szedrás-bácsi had learned of his induction as *föhadnagy* in the Kaiser Wilhelm Hussars. This was an unprecedented honour. To serve as an officer with the elite of the Magyar nobility in the country's most prestigious military regiment was a distinction for anyone, but for a Jew unheard of.

"Always clever," said Gábor, "my brother Bandi piped up. 'I know. It's your horse, isn't it, Szedrás-bácsi? Your new horse that you bought for the cavalry. Will they bring it today?' My uncle snorted because Bandi had guessed well. The pinch he gave Bandi's cheek was appreciative but, I knew from experience, painful. 'Not *my* horse, not yet. But something on four legs—no, eight—should be pulling up here soon.'

"Szedrás-bácsi's anticipation was infectious. He made broad hints and pulled at our ears. My uncle was high-strung as a thoroughbred. When he was in the room, he was the centre of attention. A fine manly figure, he looked taller than his real stature because he held himself ramrod straight. He didn't walk; he strode. He didn't converse; he declared. Out in the fields the peasants bent into their work when they heard him coming. My poor grandfather more than once had to listen to a farmer complain that Master Szedrás had expressed himself with force. They knew Grandfather was pious and good-hearted and would reach into his pocket.

"'But Szedrás, what's this!' Anyuka cried, rushing to the window after Bandi and Miki spied the ponies and raced out.

Well, of course I couldn't run in that confining corset. So, trailing behind my brothers, I heard what sounded like dismay in her voice.

"'Why the war, darling sister, the war! What better occasion could there be? The glorious war, and your brother's remarkable opportunity to serve the emperor! I want my nephews to remember!'"

"Who knows from where my Uncle Szedrás got his military vocation?" Gábor mused. "Grandfather Aron said it sprang from an ancient gene that went as far back as the defenders of Jericho. Certainly no other family member in recent memory was like him. An ancient gene had randomly surfaced, defining my Uncle Szedrás. Grandfather Aron moved heaven and earth to indulge his son's longing to serve with Hungary's best. Not because he was weak and Szedrás-bácsi too willful. Grandfather Aron was quick and shrewd, but tender-hearted. He loved his children too much. They were all of them spoiled, even my saintly mother whose passion for religion was as deep as her brother's military ambition. Grandfather Aron could deny his children—all twelve of them—nothing. My mother's obsession for the dietary laws he catered to with separate kitchens no less—one for *milchig*, the other for *fleischig*. A rebetzin could not have observed more fastidiously. Although he bought Szedrás a handsome charger to ride in the cavalry, not a day of the war would pass without Grandfather praying with tears pouring down his face for his eldest son's safety. For Uncle Lajos he bought a motor car to ferry the bigwigs between Budapest and Vienna and so stay out of active combat. Uncle Duri's exemption from the military he purchased with bribes. They had only to ask and gold poured from Grandfather Aron's pockets."

The Rákóczi Tanya as Gábor remembered it was the lap of familial love. It engendered affection that spilled like change into the grasping hands of all the children, young and old alike. Gábor felt he had been born between the cornucopious thighs of Mother Earth, between the Tigris and Euphrates as he loved to say, the very source of life.

When pressed for accuracy, though, he allowed that Grand-father Aron had entered adulthood without financial backing, and naught but a parochial education and a family legend to get him started. Gröszmann lore had it that when Itzig the Jew arrived in the Nyirség he brought with him not even a sur-name. He dusted off a spot by the side of the road, erected a rough table, and placed on it a heel of bread. From this crust, travel-weary strangers were invited to sup and restore themselves. Then they went on their way leaving, in exchange, blessings.

According to family myth, these blessings manifested them-selves tangibly in wealth. Word of Itzig's bounty by the side of the road spread to parts north and east. Aptly dubbed Grösz-mann by grateful guests, Itzig's descendants continued to live up to their moniker, big-spirited, bountiful, burgeoning. The legendary table continued to be set for strangers, even after walls and roof were built around it. The legacy of hospitality, a sweet, soul-pleasing principle, Grandfather Aron adopted as his maxim. Grandfather Aron's "nothing," Gábor permitted, consisted of a name, a legend and a reputation. Like a calling card, the name Gröszmann had preceded him through parts north and east, an ambassador of trade. Synonymous with largesse, it opened the doors of homes and inns, and it unlocked the coffers of investors. It was the legacy upon which Aron built his fortune, and he never forgot the origin of its meaning. "Like Itzig our Ances-tor," said Gábor, "the more Grandfather Aron gave away, the more the Lord saw fit to bless him." Aron's fortune appeared to Gábor to have been based on an open purse. He'd felt this kindness extended towards him and his brothers in small gifts of bonbons and tender excuses for their childish transgressions. Naturally, he added as an aside, there was Grandfather Aron's business acumen.

"The courtyard where the little team had drawn up causing such a stir and commotion among us children was the heart of the Rákóczi Tanya," Gábor recounted. "An estate of almost a thousand *holds*, the Tanya ran more like an industry than a farm, and nowhere was this more evident than in the courtyard that was its hub. Here stood not only the big house, but also the distillery, the stables, barns, outbuildings and servant quarters. So when the miniature carriage drawn by two matched ponies pulled up in front of the house, the eyes of all—bailiffs, foremen, farmhands, servants—were on the exquisite toy equipage.

"We children were excited and eager to try it out, but we couldn't help but be aware that all the eyes of our world were upon us."

The coach and pair that had drawn up in front of the big house was no mere pony cart, but a miniature replica of a carriage that might roll down the Maria Theresa Strasse in Vienna. Wincing at the aristocratic, ergo gentile, look of the rig, Liliana watched her boys pore over its perfect details: the silver-cropped whip, the shiny brass grip on the door, the polished wood running board, and the coat of arms emblazoned on the coachman's tower. The carriage was a burnished black, encasing a too-red interior that made Liliana think of a sliced-open heart. But neither silver nor red leather could outshine the two ponies. The boys stroked and patted their soft sides, exclaiming that one was as white as goose down while the other looked like night.

The shaved mane on the black pony was like the fresh military look the two older boys had sported on their return from town, shorn of their long locks a few weeks earlier. In comparison, the white pony's mane was long and luxurious. It was cunning how the ponies were a perfect contrast to one another. The brothers rubbed the bristling thatch on the black, remarking how the cropped mane made it look like the older of the two.

Their father, Wilmos, had insisted on the haircuts. "Eight years old and with his condition especially, Gabi needs to feel some respect."

Liliana's eyes had filled. "Dearest, have I been too selfish? Lord forgive me if I've contributed to our child's pain."

Miki had made no objection when his older brothers were taken to town. He spent the day with édes Anyuka learning his letters. Since then she ran her hands more freely through the silky strands on his head.

At the window, Liliana worried about Gabi. Would her boy muster enough strength to hold back his hardy brother without collapsing in exhaustion? She hadn't the heart to bring him in before he had driven the carriage, but it would hurt his brave spirit if he crumpled out there in front of everyone. Knowing Gabi, he was probably trying to find a way to assert his right as eldest without offending Bandi. Taking his time to think required endurance, however, and time was what Gabi lacked. The traitorous thought startled her with a stab. It was as near as she had ever come to acknowledging her son's disease. "Condition" they called it amongst themselves; "weakness" was how they referred to it publicly. Only once had Wilmos mentioned to her the name that hung like a sword over their heads since his consultation with the famous Budapest specialist. "Weakness, dear sir!" The Budapest doctor had thrust the diagnosis at him. "Sir, your son suffers from tuberculosis—tuberculosis of the spine." It had come as a shock. Not only was the disease deadly; it was the affliction of the peasants and the poor. How could such an ailment have found purchase within their enlightened household?

The little ponies dipped their heads as though politely urging the two boys to finish their business. Gabi felt the familiar softness in his legs. It was as if his back was an anvil crushing their strength. His family called his back weak, but to him it felt more like an iron-cast weight that bore him down. On bad days as he lay on the special mold attached to his bed to keep him from shifting position, his back pinned him in place, a boulder far stronger than his childish limbs could budge.

He pressed his argument with Bandi, but the words came out panting. "The coachman doesn't mount until *all* the passengers are settled. Only then," he managed to stress meaningfully, "can he safely loosen the reins."

Noticing his brother flag, Bandi instantly gave Gabi his point. He climbed into the carriage without another word. Anyuka would be distraught if Gabi collapsed out here in plain sight of everyone.

"Stay on your side," he warned Miki roughly, concerned he

might have pushed Gabi too far. "And don't go leaning way out. After all, it's not Csapati up there in the box."

Miki giggled. He pointed at Gabi and rolled the corner of his mouth like a camel's, imitating the way Csapati sucked his long moustache. Bandi gave him a cuff, but laughed.

Csapati the coachman looked on from the stable, absent-mindedly chewing his moustache in just the way Miki mimicked. The workings of his jaw conveyed the extent of his disapproval. That Master Szedrás had so little sense as to spend a fortune on this toy was typical, but that the rest of them would stand by and let the crippled boy endanger his healthy brothers was less than he expected from them. The trap was a plaything perhaps, but it was hitched to two creatures that however well trained were live and unpredictable. Look at that, the young master could hardly haul himself up into the coachman's tower even though it was barely three feet from the ground.

Liliana noticed too, but she refused to credit what she saw. Why, just last week Gabi was able to stand through most of the Shabbat prayers, *davening* like a little man. They adhered strictly to the regime set out by the doctor in nearby Debrecen, from whom they had sought a second opinion. He had assured them that with the support of the corset and the plaster cast on his bed, Gabi's back would straighten. She would not believe what her eyes told her. Surely Gabi's condition could not have so deteriorated in a few short weeks that he could barely manage two steps up into the box on the carriage. The Lord who had spared Abraham his Isaac would not take from her her first-born child.

Szedrás stewed. The scene was not playing as he'd imagined. He had pictured his nephews in the beautifully appointed replica, but with handsome Bandi up in the box and Gabi's disability disguised inside the carriage. The striking equipage would first, at a princely pace, circle the great courtyard, then Bandi would urge the ponies into a canter and weave them masterfully between the buildings, demonstrating to all who looked on what this family had become. But there was Gabi weak as a worm, teetering over the reins. It was an unbearable mockery. "He's going to make a laughingstock of us!" Szedrás exploded.

Gabi sat on the box precariously, almost swaying from the effort it had taken to get up there. His hand clasped the reins like a life line. He had not realized how tightly he held on until his hand throbbed inside the leather casing. When the ponies tugged, the leather bit his skin. Poor creatures, Csapati thought, it was a wonder the boy didn't cut their mouths, he leaned on the reins so heavily.

"Let go," Bandi prompted from inside the carriage. Gabi knew he should unwrap his hand from the leather bandage, but even this seemed an effort.

Gábor's voice dropped somewhat, as though he were about to say something off the record. "I had for a while felt my strength fading, but a child does not understand. I obediently surrendered myself to the regime of the corset and the cast that the Debrecen doctor said would heal my condition. Naturally I believed in what my parents thought best.

"The surgeon in Budapest whom my dear father had first consulted was a specialist in pediatric orthopedics, but what he had prescribed was so risky and impractical my parents recoiled from the procedure. I was to be brought to him every few months and he would drain the pus from the abscess in my spine. 'And how exactly, Honourable Doctor, do you propose to drain the abscess?' my father had asked, blanching before he even heard the response. But the famous doctor guaranteed nothing. Not how many times it would be necessary to pierce my spinal column, nor a complete recovery. He made no assurances.

"My beloved parents chose the less radical treatment recommended by the second doctor in nearby Debrecen. It was wartime, no simple journey to Budapest. There were long delays and disruptions along the rails, with military transports taking precedence over civilian travel. My parents made the reasonable decision.

"I felt my strength wane, but a boy entrusts himself to his elders. My mother believed fervently in the usefulness of the corset. At that time any form of surgery was feared like the plague and to be avoided at any cost; yes, any. My grandmother, Grandfather Aron's beloved wife, had left him a widower with twelve motherless children because she refused to let an aggravated hernia be operated on. And Grandfather Aron himself would in due course succumb to diabetes he treated with no more than the mineral waters at the Carlsbad spa. Before their eyes I withered until finally, in desperation, my beloved father wrapped me in blankets and almost carried me, alternating between horse and buggy, and rail, and lastly from the outskirts of Budapest by motor car, to the great surgeon in the capital who brutally accused him: 'You call yourself a father, Mr. Weisz. In my eyes you are a murderer.'"

"But as you can see," Gábor resumed a heavier tone, "my dear father did not kill me with a tenderness that had only tried to spare me pain. For from then on we travelled regularly to Budapest, wartime notwithstanding, both of us imagining all the way the dreadful needle. He did not kill me after all, for the famous Budapest surgeon was not famous for nothing. In Budapest today the clinic is called the National Children's Institute, but people still refer to it as the Berek Klinika. They no longer care who Károly Berek was, but here, a continent, an ocean and a lifetime away, an indebted former patient remembers."

"Gee-yup!"

"Fool!" Csapati spat into his moustache. Szedrás had sprung from the house, spurring the carriage to a start with a smart smack to the hindquarters of the white pony. The eager heads of the animals arched forward as they broke suddenly into step, jerking Gabi from the seat he had just laboriously gained. From the house it looked to Liliana that her child dangled from the reins like an entangled marionette. Her heart leapt into her mouth, displacing words of prayer. Realizing his error in judgement, Szedrás tried to intercept the animals, but they were strong and quick and relieved to get going.

"Stay down! Down!" Csapati shouted at Bandi, who tried from inside the carriage to grab hold of his older brother.

"Down!" Csapati yelled, running from the stable towards the bolting ponies. He knew the carriage must be too light for the combined strength of the animals, and would tip like a rowboat if rocked from within.

But Bandi heard nothing over the whir of the wheels. He stretched out for Gabi, then pitched sideways when, headed off by Csapati, the animals slowed and veered into a turn. Liliana watched helplessly as the carriage tipped over, spilling her children. Szedrás caught Bandi as he hurtled out and hit the ground running. Little Miki rolled into the dust. But Gabi and the ponies were still bound together. Liliana didn't remember leaving the house, but she was standing over Gabi, whose little hands were tangled in the reins. Her own hands fluttered. She couldn't bring herself to look at her son, only his trapped hands. If she looked at him he might be broken, his delicate limbs twisted unnaturally. He might be bleeding. As long as she didn't look at him, she could still think of him as whole. She concentrated on his hands. She had to do something about his hands. Someone was screaming but she refused to hear. Trembling, the maternal fingers unwound her child's from their noose. Then, stopping her ears with silence, she followed on rubber legs while Csapati carried the sobbing boy back to the house.

That was the first of the tumbles taken by all the children in the család. The pony carriage became a popular attraction to visiting cousins. It balanced well enough when hitched to just one of the ponies, but the children couldn't resist their beautiful pairing, nor the added thrill of going as fast as possible without tipping over. Home on leave from the emperor's Hussars, Uncle Szedrás was often rewarded with the sight of a pretty, ringletted cousin, the ribbons of her straw hat flying behind her as with one hand she clasped her hat, and with the other steadied herself on the rattling door of the racing carriage. Little Miki's ringlets, too, whipped behind him as he flicked the reins or snapped the silver-handled lash above his head.

Gábor drew meaning from his accident, as he was inclined to do from all his experiences. "I look back on my carriage accident as the first intimation of my family's slide from grace, but it was, for me personally, a blessing. As she followed the coachman who carried me in his arms, my dear mother had to admit in her heart the seriousness of my disease. Bruised and terrified, from that point on, I stopped hiding my discomfort. It seemed to the family that my condition had worsened with alarming speed. The uncles and aunts openly referred to me as 'poor darling.'

"During my early years a polite but recurring debate had waged between my parents over how we boys should be educated. It came swiftly to an end. There was no question now of sending me, the cripple, away to school. And because the natural inclination within the család was to do things 'en bloc,' so to speak, my brothers too stayed on the Tanya.

"Talmud-Torah scholars were available by the dozen. Grandfather Aron had his pick of the best. Soon a brilliant tutor and his family were established in a Tanya farmhouse to teach the Weisz boys the ancient wisdom of our people. For almost a decade this was the only formal learning from which we benefited. My beloved father had cherished a dream of a secular education for his sons, but édes Anyuka mistrusted gentile thought. Her cause was furthered by our studying at home, since secular scholars did not wander, hungry, around the countryside like itinerant yeshiva bochers. No professor could be found to meet my father's specifications.

"During that childhood decade, the Great War raged and reduced the Austro-Hungarian empire. An aborted Bolshevik uprising forced the család to abandon the Tanya for a brief period, and seek refuge with relations in the capital. The Romanians occupied the country temporarily, which we took note of principally through an eruption of my Uncle Szedrás's outrage that resulted in a duel between him and one of the local Romanian constabulary and, to smooth things out, the near depletion of Grandfather Aron's reserves, already taxed heavily by wartime demands. But it was as though history stormed around us while we enjoyed a perpetual calm. For us boys, tutored and raised at home, childhood was an arbour of familial doting. We felt that no matter what went on outside, we were protected and blessed.

"It is best not to ask too many questions. My devout mother held that the Lord would not take me. And she was right. He did not. But it was my beloved father's faith, finally, in secular learning that overruled their fear of surgery and had him rush me to the surgeon who saved my life. I was saved. My life endured, the one that had hung by a thread. All the others, sturdy stalks that bloomed and bore fruit that was the finest of its kind, the others burned to the ground.

"Perhaps Abraham's love for Isaac was a big mistake. The Lord required a sacrifice, and He would have it one way or another."

Looking directly at me, Gábor demanded, as though I had challenged him, "Why did the család not know? Why did we brothers not realize if we were so smart? And we were. Dreadfully clever. My beloved father in due course achieved his dream for our education. An illustrious instructor, tanár-úr Hász, was lured from the Debrecen föiskola—secondary school—no doubt induced by a handsome offer from my grandfather, who indulged my father like one of his own. By then I was a young man of fifteen who had long since discarded the corset and could tramp the Tanya fields like any other gentleman farmer. To Hász-tanár's credit, within four years the Weisz brothers, all three of us, were accepted, despite the quotas restricting Jewish enrolment, into the Debrecen Académia. Even I with my tone-deaf ear became more fluent in Latin than the gentile students, for the entrance requirements to the Académia were much stricter for Jews. Very smart. Eventually all three of us graduated with honours, and Miki went on to Vienna to earn his Doctorate of Law.

"The name Szemes was a curse. We prided ourselves on clear-sightedness, the ability to see past the limitations of sand and poverty to a vision of an irrigated oasis in the desert. But it blinded us from seeing what is evident even to the eyes of a child, what you can see for yourself—that we should have used whatever influence we enjoyed to make the sacrifice. We should

have given up everything and run for our lives. Indeed we were
szemes, the kind of corn fodder that is turned back into the
earth to enrich it.

"Csapati the coachman said something to me once that I will
never forget. By then he was old and bald except for the rag of
a moustache he still chewed like a nagging riddle. I had found
my way home. The skin that hung on my bones was good only
for lice. At the beginning of February I had left the Tanya
for what I assumed would be my last service in slave labour.
The Russians were on our doorstep. The Americans had landed
in the west. Germany would get squeezed from both sides. My
little daughter Clárika hung from my neck and I felt her breath
on my cheek sweet and light and more perfect than a kiss. For
the first time since the outbreak of war my heart didn't crack
as I held her. The end was in sight. 'When you come back ...,'
she whispered, but I didn't let her finish. I wouldn't let her
make her promise, because the promise was mine. I hugged her
with a kind of joy, promising it would be the last time I would
have to tell her good-bye.

"Winter was yet to come when I returned in November. There
had been neither spring nor summer. The seasons had stopped.
The land lay fallow. Since mid-March I had received no response
to my sporadic letters. No more letters reached me listing the
family's confiscations and shortages. No reports of my brothers
at their labour camp postings. No childish drawings. I could tell
I had stumbled onto Tanya ground because the soil when I
stooped to touch it was hard and cracked, not crumbly as Nyirség
sand. The Tanya was bare except for a bent figure also scratching in the dust. It rose to the sound of my shuffling approach,
thinking in that chewing way with its mouth.

" 'Csapati, don't you know me?' I asked.

" 'Know you, Master Gabi? Who knows anyone now? Recognize you? Perhaps.'

"I opened my hands. Speechlessly I indicated the Tanya,
afraid to ask what had happened here.

"He raised an eyebrow, squinting with shrewd intelligence
and trying to guess what I knew to be fact and what I only

surmised. I knew the Germans in retreat had hauled away a last catch in their deadly net. All trains had headed east. My labour detachment too had advanced towards Germany. The relentless eastwards march showed me I had no alternative but to desert. I escaped, but that is another story for another day. Few were as lucky. Bandi, my beloved brother, I later learned suffocated in a copper mine on the Yugoslav border. I found out too that Miki, the család's pride, home on an unexpected leave, was rounded up with the rest. You ask me why I am always so gloomy at this time of year. This is it. There is a period before winter when the earth is barren, not festooned in snow and ice, nor brimming with harvest. Merely over and done with. It was at that time of year that I returned to the Tanya. Neither autumn nor winter, but what over here they call aptly the fall.

"This was when Csapati said the words I can still hear plainly, especially their sly innuendo.

"'Not many are left around here,' he said, 'not since it pleased you all to take off.'

"*Pleased us*. He said it *pleased* us. He was afraid, you see, that I might hold him accountable in some way. *Pleased* us to take off. As though we had left of our own volition. If only God had so willed.

"*Why?* Why, you want to know, did we not leave before it was too late? Across Europe Jews were dying. We did not acknowledge it, but we knew. In Hungary it was different. We felt protected by an independent government. Hungary was not occupied by the Germans until the very end. Hungary supported Germany, but stopped short of the final solution. In the desert of Nazi Europe, until the very end, Hungary was an oasis in a manner of speaking. When the Lord surveyed what He created, He found it was good. Why would we have questioned His judgement?

"You think you are smart, still a child but already you think you know everything. Then answer me this. Do you think we'd be here now—me, you, your sister and your mother—in a land thick with forests—if you children hadn't sprouted from the ashes of the dead?

"I left my homeland for more reasons, probably, than even I can guess, stripped like my ancestor Itzig to nothing. And I came with a new family to a strange land, with only the legacy I carried in my heart. I brought with me my father's name, a name I loved because there was nothing *grósz*, nothing grand, about it."

Before the War that brought about the Fall of the Jews of Europe and the Rákóczi Tanya, as well as the failure of Love, Gábor said there was Light. I imagined a red dawn glowing in the east. A world emerged on that horizon. Under its sun a small paradise bloomed that was heaven and earth together. And in that world there was Life, not just its shadow, Memory. Who was I to question?

THE

COUNTY

OF

BIRCHES

My mother, Sári, met my father, Gábor, in a schoolhouse in
September 1945. She sat with the women at the back of the
schoolroom that smelled of dust and dry leaves and a trace
of chalk, like ash. The evocation of ash was almost sensual.
Powdery and soft as child's hair, and that unreal. Murmuring
was subdued, because of those who weren't there.

The young men improvising the Rosh Hashanah service sat
up front behind a lectern. One by one they stood to read the
prayers they knew by heart, avoiding the eyes of those who had
gathered.

"And this one?" Sári whispered. "Who is the one pulling his
ear like a sidelock? Kramer, you say, from Nyirbátor? And the
one with red hair ... ?"

She had drifted to her first husband's county when she had
found no one of her own in Beregszász. In any event, the con-
ference in Yalta had traded her hometown to the Soviets. She
left while the boundaries were just dotted and pencilled in, as
empty-handed as she'd arrived. What could she have taken that

would have survived the war, a bolt of cloth from her mother's shop?

"What about this one, the big one? Weisz? Weisz, you say? What Weisz? Which Weisz? From where—Vaja? The Vaja Weiszes? No." No, János had never mentioned any relations from that village.

Sári Friedlander Weisz shared Gábor's name by marriage. She would have passed him over like the rest had she not learned from the other women that he was head of local JOINT, where those who came back sought assistance. Gábor Weisz was the man to see about finding János.

Sári observed him reading. The voice tuneless but proficient, round head nodding to an age-old cadence, thick fingers turning the page ahead of his words, just like any old-fashioned davening Jew. He couldn't have been more different from her János. Weisz. The same name, and from the same county. It was a cruel coincidence that another Weisz, but of no shared blood, belonged to this sad scrap of earth.

The town of Nyíregyháza where Sári met Gábor is named for the birch tree, like many of the cities and hamlets of the plain in northeastern Hungary. This flatland is actually more distinguished by the acacias that grow profusely in its sandy soil than by anything we North Americans would recognize as birch. Nonetheless, my father's region abounds in tributes to the white-barked tree. The Nyírség, it is called—the state of being birch—and its towns reflect this birchness in name if nothing else: Nyírmada, Nyírgyulaj, Nyírbátor, Nyírvásvári, Nyírmegges, Nyírjákó, Nyírvaja. The birch names are as ubiquitous as they are unpronounceable in English.

I begin here, when, after the service, Gábor passed through the congregation clasping hands. Round-faced Gábor, his nose long and sorrowful, his brown eyes initially shrinking from something so lovely as this woman with hair she threw back like a mare tossing its mane, accepted the hand Sári held out first. Sári Friedlander Weisz deliberately flaunted her hair as though it had grown thick and rich, long and dark, out of defiance. Her inborn vanity had not been expunged by near death from gas and starvation. She was a woman who had grown back hardier and harder, like a rosebush pruned close to the quick. Her hair had been fair before it was shaved.

I imagine myself conceived when my mother, tossing back her hair, felt my father's eyes upon her. Light-sensitive eyes that had sworn off joy. Deeply impressionable, they drank in her hair, brown and unfettered like his first wife Miri's had been only in the privacy of their bedroom, and her legs like a doe's slim and long, and her hand outstretched like a man's.

I begin at this point when my father's heart rekindles, though theoretically I go back further, before the great conflagration that reduced the numbers of his family from over a hundred to fewer than twenty, to the very beginning in fact of what we know of his ancestry, the pious vagabond without a surname called Itzig the Jew, which may have been a name generic to every Jew in the countryside. Itzig the Jew dragging his caftan in the dust of the Hungarian countryside at the end of the eighteenth century. I also hark back to the vineyards where my mother grew up and she and her six siblings played hide and seek, though it was forbidden to touch or trample the valuable fruit. (Among seven children, there are always a few young and small enough to wriggle belly down along the furrows, and fast enough to flee the raised fists of the field hands when they are discovered.) The story really starts with them, because who my parents once were and where they came from is a sum I repeatedly figure, trying to calculate how it adds up to me and my sister.

Like any child, most of all I care about the I. The I that clamours to speak for itself. This I owes less to the piety of generations of orthodox Jews or to the mercantile candour that characterized my mother's family than it does—its very inception—to the war that wedded them and to which it became reluctant heir.

I knew this war like I knew the pale hand that held the spoon to my mouth. A hand moderately proportioned, distinguished by its smoothness and the incipient arthritic swell of its knuckles. I felt these joints when I played with her wedding band, working the ring up and over the first knuckle. Even the second one arched slightly, causing the ring to skin its surface. I have always known the war like I knew the impatient withdrawal of that hand if food was not taken quickly enough or if the ring slipped and fell from my stubby fingers. I have never not known of the war, though I don't recall hearing about it for the first time any more than I remember the first chime of my mother's voice or kiss of fresh air.

The war came to me with all that is good. It dawned on me like my own sweet flesh and buds of toes and the bright gold band that lay on the soft pads of my palm.

My mother's marriage, the one before Gábor, was hardly more than a courtship. Promenading arm-in-arm along the *korzo*, she in her smart suit and box hat, her military man uniformed, they made a decorative couple. People mated during the disastrous decade. People stepped out and showed off. They would wake up one day and the nightmare would be over. A beautiful girl like Sári, her parents reasoned, would need to be married. My mother dwelt on that, the promenading, the handsome figure they cut as a pair. It was all she had to tell us, all there was to that match.

And that on her wedding night she was slipped under the wire of the labour camp. She'd say that matter-of-factly. On her three-week honeymoon she was smuggled into the camp nightly. *Under the wire of the labour camp.*

Sári, my mother, who squirmed away impatiently whenever Gábor gave her fanny a friendly pat. Sári who, kissing me goodnight, pulled both my arms from under the bedclothes and pressed them firmly over the blankets, admonishing me to keep them that way. Sári who educated me early in the decorum of intimacy with the cryptic warning, "Remember, it's always the man who takes and the woman who gives." Her stance was prudish and ingenuous, as though she had never been touched by men's hands.

Yet every night for three weeks, she had allowed herself to be smuggled onto János's pallet. Risking military discipline, they made a love that must have been memorable. Love, among the coughs and groans and gases of male strangers. He waited for her in the dark beside the wire fence he and his friends had clipped and disguised, then pulled her through the dark into the barracks that smelled of boots and sweat. This young woman who had accepted his kisses coquettishly, always drawing back, who had lived sheltered in her parents' home, never exposed to danger. In that animal kingdom of men and their fear of death, I assume he used humour to disarm her. *Humour.* Because what we knew about my mother's first husband, we had heard from Gábor.

My father described János Weisz as a professional soldier, an officer in fact, who had served as captain in the Magyar army. Stripped by the so-called "Jewish Laws" of his rank and career, János Weisz was conscripted into the labour service in the fall of 1941, just like Gábor and his brother Bandi, agronomists by profession, and their lawyer-brother Miklós. They were thrown together with village boys so poor and unschooled my father and his brothers had to take them in hand, show them what part of the boot to polish, simple village Jews whose main skill was the practice of Jewish tradition. János Weisz became their natural leader. When the actual sergeant turned out to be a Hungarian peasant much like themselves, pulled from his hut and put in charge of a regiment, no one questioned the authority of János Weisz over the ragtail band. The military officer was relieved to lie low in the local café.

The first labour service bore little resemblance to what would follow. As the war progressed, licence with life was taken increasingly. But when the labour service was first established, Hungarian Jews were emboldened to believe that if this was all that was going to happen—this and their restriction from professions and owning land—if what was to be taken from them fell short of breath, they could bear it. Labour service would kill Bandi in the copper mines of Bor and abandon János Weisz on the Russian front, but it saved my father from Buchenwald.

Gábor respected János Weisz. János was not a big man, but his military bearing gave him stature. He was younger than

Gábor but, Gábor said, you could see that he was a man of the world, not easily intimidated. My father was impressed by the distance János Weisz kept from the rest of them, for the sake of authority.

Enlistment took place a few weeks before Jewish New Year. For many of the men in the troop this would be their first Rosh Hashanah away from home. Business and education had led Jews of the monied class out into the world, but it was usual for poor Jews of the countryside to live their lives in one village. Observance of the High Holy Days was through prayer and strict abstention from work. The village Jews assumed that the Lord would see to it that His Law, as intrinsic as the laws of nature, would prevail. Tension mounted as the High Holy Days approached and the Lord had not indicated what they should do.

János Weisz became aware that the poor Jews in his company had started looking on him as the unlikely instrument of the Lord. They were fearful and uncertain, bowed beneath centuries of religious tradition and secular authority. János Weisz knew the ways of their military and Christian masters. They didn't accept him as a real Jew; he was too worldly, too tainted by outside influences. But in his own way he was enough like them to understand their dilemma. János Weisz grew aloof. He withdrew and ate alone, giving no indication of how he would direct them on upcoming Rosh Hashanah.

Gábor and his brothers were orthodox Jews, but their God appreciated extenuating circumstances. They would risk His wrath before that of their taskmasters. Gábor sympathized with János Weisz, whose authority was unofficial at best. The slightest leniency on János Weisz's part, or suggestion that he was sparing the Jews, might unleash upon them all some devil sent to teach them a lesson, and on himself a personal penalty. But when a delegation begged Gábor to appeal to János Weisz to permit them to observe the Holy Day with respect, Gábor could not bring himself to refuse. He saw their beardless faces and heads shaved in military fashion, so incongruous with the pious stoop of their shoulders and bends of their noses and melancholy eyes, and he felt for them a deep pity. These people were helpless without their customs.

On *erev* Rosh Hashanah, the eve of the holiday, Gábor approached János Weisz. The mood in the barracks was heavy with dread. János Weisz lost his patience. Had someone died here? Which one of them had been beaten recently, or received a bullet in the head? Which one of them had passed a day without eating? What were these fools mooning about? Did they not realize? Did they not know that Jews elsewhere in Europe were dying? Now here was Gábor Weisz, a man of good sense who should know better; what did Weisz expect of him?

"János," Gábor began, "the men are deeply distressed at having to work and desecrate this Holy Day."

"Is that so?" The reply was curt and impassive. "Let them make their apologies to the Lord then."

Gábor was surprised and offended. He was a man of social standing, accustomed to respect in the Jewish community. Shrugging, he returned to the others.

Rosh Hashanah dawned, a day like any other. And as on any other day, János Weisz marched his men into the woods.

Ten days later, on Yom Kippur, no one appealed to the Jew in János Weisz. True, Gábor recalled, the mood among the company was funereal. But no one suggested observing the Day of Days. Those who chose would fast and pray while they worked.

János Weisz called up his company on Yom Kippur and marched them out. Each man carried his axe and his pack. At home, they would have walked the shortest distance to *shul*. They would have spent the day in prayer neither drinking nor eating until the first star appeared in the heavens. This Yom Kippur morning was cold and clear. The sun rose in a cloudless sky, brightening the firmament. Ordinarily it would have been the kind of fall day they might have liked being outside. The trees would wear long shadows; the men would take in the cold air, and watch clouds of breath affirm that they were alive. But because it was Yom Kippur, the boots marched into the forest bearing them like husks.

The discontent, unvoiced, was nonetheless pronounced. Day after day their company of Jews had felled timber to meet a daily quota. The military officer had come out once or twice to keep up a semblance of command, but regularly he was more than content to leave the company's direction to Weisz. Far from the front, and performing menial back-up services, their company had received only tertiary attention from the authorities. All Rosh Hashanah day they had wielded their axes. And if János Weisz had called just a fifteen-minute break for them to respectfully say a few prayers, there would have been none to know the difference. When his men looked at János Weisz, they did not see his military training. That meant nothing to them. What they saw was an apostate Jew, and he affected them with horror.

At noon of the holiest day of the year, János Weisz gave the order to stop. The axes ceased swinging. The men looked up. No one pulled bread from his pack. János Weisz barked, "Quota met! Company, dismissed!" The men stood irresolutely, unsure of what was meant by the command. Clearly they had not achieved the day's requirement. "Dismissed!" János Weisz shouted again.

Gábor summoned his two younger brothers. Arms around each other, they turned to face east to the Holy Land, as did each member of the company. Then, not daring to murmur their prayers aloud, they began to sway to an ingrained measure. Some had hats; others tore leaves from the trees to cover their heads, not to appear bareheaded before the Lord.

Outside, under the sun and among the trees, they celebrated the Holy One, praised be He. Gábor said later that the sun's rays had poured over them. In all his life, he never had—and never would again—feel so tangibly the presence of God. As a boy in the synagogue of his paternal grandfather he had not felt so near to the Deity. Nagyapa Weisz with his prophet's face and passion had awed the boy with the force of his faith. Yet here in the woods, in the open air, Gábor felt the Creator in His element. Gábor felt loved by God.

"What do you mean, Apu?" I asked, hearing this story for

the third or fourth time. "What do you mean, 'loved by God'? How did He love you different from the others? Why you, Apu, why did God love you and not János Weisz or Bandi-bácsi or Miklós-bácsi, or your wife Miri-néni or your baby Clárika?"

"I don't say God loved only me, where do you get that?" he answered testily. "I say that I felt at that moment that indeed God loved me. He loved us all to pour His glory over us. To let us worship Him so purely out in the open amid His creations. He could only love us to create for us such a wonderful moment. Terror and sorrow and loss transformed into the glory of God. He must have loved us to create for us such a moment. And I felt He loved me. That He was there with me, beside me, warming me with the breath of His love."

While the company of Jews prayed, János Weisz struck his axe. Throughout the afternoon, he maintained a steady rhythm. That is how the sergeant found them. From a distance, a single axe stroke did not sound thin. But as the sergeant neared it would have become evident that not everyone could be working. Even so, he was taken by surprise at the sight awaiting him when he came through the trees. Men scattered in the woods, swaying silently, lost in their own private worlds like inmates in an asylum for lunatics. One madman swinging an axe. A company of mindless mutes, facing east, swaying on its heels.

The sergeant was a thick-armed peasant. Having neither money nor education nor aristocratic name, he would never have reached the rank of officer in normal times. Some officers with little experience compensated with excessive brutality.

"Weisz! What's the meaning of this?" he demanded.

János Weisz had laid down his axe, Gábor said. He stood smartly at attention to answer his commanding officer.

"Sir," he said distinctly and without hesitation, "the men are overworked, Sir. They need to rest."

"And who decided this? Who said they are tired? Who gave them permission to rest?"

"I did, Sir."

Stalled by the authority in his subordinate's response, the

sergeant wavered indecisively until he was struck by a baffling observation.

"On their feet! They rest on their feet?"

"Yes, Sir," said János Weisz without blinking or expression. "That's how they rest, Sir—Jews. Like horses."

"*Like horses,*" Gábor said. "János Weisz said 'like horses.'" And Gábor would chuckle slyly. He was not a man given to laughter. When he did laugh, it was always with some guilt. "*Like horses. Do you see?*" Not one of us enjoyed the joke more than Gábor. It was always fresh for him.

No one had laughed in the woods. No one moved for some moments. The silence was complete, palpable with the sense of impending reprisal. But the sergeant retreated without comment.

My mother listened quietly whenever Gábor told us the story of the Yom Kippur woods. She never said impatiently, as she did to so many of my father's anecdotes, "We know that one already." The rapt way in which I followed Gábor's tales usually made her fidget or get up to make a phone call. But she would listen to this story, told always the same way, ending always with Gábor's chuckle, "Like horses." My mother recognized the humour. She knew the man who wooed a young bride inside a barracks that was a portico to death, the man who could find something funny in these circumstances. At the time she had understood János's recklessness as ardour, but Gábor's story showed a man who defied the inexorable march of history by slowing it down a few paces. As Gábor wove the scene of the Erdelyi Woods, Sári listened. So this was the man who had pleasured her in the dark. This was the man with whom she might have spent her life.

Gábor survived four labour services altogether. It was during a discharge, as he was about to board the train that would take him home to where his wife, Miri, and their child had moved to be with his parents, that his path literally crossed that of his fellow serviceman. János Weisz was disembarking. He had been called up to re-enlist. The two men greeted each other warmly, hands clasping in the steaming stench and roar of the station.

And how have you fared in these lousy times?

They had not been close, not friends. After the Yom Kippur episode, János Weisz had maintained his reserve. But when they met in the Nagyvárad train station, János and Gábor felt a warmth for each other that might have blossomed into friendship in another clime. They shook hands, and Gábor clapped the other man's shoulder.

"So, you're on your way then. Do you know where they're sending you?"

"Who knows anything?" János replied. "But you're going home. That's what matters. Look, I'm not doing so bad. Let me show you."

Gábor was anxious to board. At home they were waiting for him. Miri had written that the child, Clárika, had started to read since he'd last seen her. She had taught herself her letters, and not yet four years old. They would be waiting in the carriage sent to meet his train.

János Weisz pulled something from his breast pocket. Grinning, he handed it to Gábor.

"She's a beauty, isn't she? We've just been engaged."

Gábor said he didn't take much notice of the photograph. It was a studio shot that revealed little more than a pretty face. He glanced at the photograph of Sári Friedlander courteously. He was glad for János Weisz. You had to go on living, believing that one day the world would turn itself right side up.

"I wish you one hundred and twenty years of happiness," Gábor said, using a Yiddish expression.

They had parted, one going home and the other away, one east and the other west. But they didn't end up at different destinations. Inscrutable the ways of the Lord that bestowed and denied, filled a moment with meaning and discarded human life. Their paths eventually met rather than crossed. They joined at the woman who would bear their name.

János Weisz returned to Hungary from the Soviet Union in June of 1948, when my sister, Lili, was seven months old. Sári and Gábor had known of his whereabouts for a short while. They were lovers at the time János was traced to a camp for prisoners of war, as the first prisoners were released by the Russians and began to trickle home, bringing with them the names of others.

Sári lost her bearings when János wrote to say he was coming home. She had given him up with the others for dead. How could he be alive if everyone else who had belonged to her was done for or gone? She had been deserted by everyone. Mamuka. Apuka. Her sisters, too: Toni, Netti, Erzsike, all her older sisters dead. Her brother Laci had escaped to England to avoid the labour service draft. Izi, her other brother, was pioneering in Palestine. Only Sári and her youngest sister, Cimi, remained. The dead were all dead. They were a vast collective. She was numb at the thought of them. Them, the solid crowd of them. When János broke from the ranks of the dead, the whole company crumpled into separate, excruciating parts.

Gábor and Sári weren't married. Without death certificates for their spouses, they could not legally marry for seven years. This allowed for the lost to be found, the departed to return, for time to sort the living from the dead. They were not officially joined, and now János was said to be alive when Sári considered someone else in every way her husband.

She had no idea what her parents would have had her do. No one had taught her the rules for this contingency. Where were Mamuka and Apuka when she needed their guidance most? How could they have left her? What would they tell her was right? Right for her. Right for János, and right for this man they had never met but who looked to her as a plant looks up at the sun and drinks the rain. She was distracted by rage and loss. Cimi was no help. Cimi was starving somewhere in the south of the country, with a Chassidic boy she had picked up like a stray cat. Sári screamed at Gábor to keep away.

Gábor found a rabbi—most likely a reasonable proxy, a young man who was once a rabbinical student, perhaps—and they built a *chupah*, the ceremonial canopy used in Jewish weddings. He told Sári: What did the state matter? They would be joined as Jews, they would become man and wife in the eyes of the Lord.

"And János?"

Gábor, essentially a conservative man, did not even attempt to overlook the affront to decency posed by his displacement of János. János was his burden, another twist of fate to Gábor's right arm.

"János will know it couldn't be helped," he sighed.

Sári married Gábor, older than her by thirteen years, the same age difference there had been between Sári and her eldest sister, Toni, in whose house she used to set the table and rock the baby. She would care for her own children as she had learned to nurse that baby who had been in Sári's girlhood the best of toys. Gábor had lost a child, too, also a little girl. Sári saw in Gábor someone who might span the chasm between her parents and her present. He was the bridge she crossed to bind the broken pieces of her life.

János had written for the first time from the Soviet Union. He wrote three identical letters, sending them in care of the JOINT offices in Budapest, in Munkács and in Nyiregyháza, the places Sári would most likely have gone back to. Sári responded, telling him of her new circumstances. She asked for his forgiveness.

No further news came from János until just before his return journey. Lili was a newborn. Sári wrote back that it was no use. But János persisted. He wrote that in the black pit of his deprivations he had thought of her and the darkness that had woven them together. He was coming home to her and to the baby, it didn't matter whose. He wanted her and he wanted the baby and he wanted them to begin. They had never had the chance to even start their life together. They'd never known what it was like to live as man and wife.

She answered that she was now the wife of another.

He wrote a last time once he was back in the country. János said he bore Sári no ill. The man she had favoured was a decent man, János recognized that. He wished them well.

As children Lili and I knew of our parents' first spouses as we knew of all their lost relatives. The card came every holiday season from another world, somewhere called Argentina:

"Best wishes, János." It was Gábor who responded, not Sári, signing on behalf of us all.

It puzzled me, the Nyírség, the county where my parents met. Why was it named for birches? When I asked him, Gábor would shrug. No, he would say, birches could never have grown there. Acacias were indigenous. Acacias in the Nyírség, the county of birches. The Nyírség became for me a place of mind against which our real acacia world would never measure up.

Gábor and Sári were plain people, something belied in the storybook concurrence of their encounter. They worked, raised their children, tended their garden, socialized little. They cared about family, tradition and security. But their story was heroic. This discrepancy irked me. The circumstances of their past imbued them with a grandeur that didn't fit. They were ennobled by tragic events, and elevated further when these events were shaped through telling. Gábor's stories grafted meaning to their lives. There was a point always to his anecdotes, as though history has form we have only to uncover. Caught up in the story, I learned to expect meaning that makes sense of the vicissitudes of time.

Gábor often said that the finger of God pointed him the way out of each brush with death—the finger of God, because he was not an intuitive man, nor one given to notions beyond reason, and because he would never attribute to himself any special good sense that was not shared by other members of his family. Gábor believed in the finger of God, because he had to explain somehow the chance of his survival. And I believed in it too; otherwise why was I here? What I figured was that for some reason or other I had to happen. Those people and their world must have been misconceived. God had made a mistake, brushed off the chalkboard, and begun again. Otherwise the tally didn't add up. My father depicted an earlier world that was a golden era of wealth and community and insoluble family bonds. The glory, and most of the happiness, predated me. Only cataclysm could have brought about my parents' union. And whatever for? Why would that have been?

There's a photograph of me before we left Hungary. I am

standing in a field, on unsteady legs wrapped in ribbed leggings. I am hatless, and my few wisps of hair have been gathered in a spout on top of my head. My expression wavers between a frown and a smile. I have been crying, says my mother, because I don't want to be photographed. The long grasses of the field bend in the breeze. I still have it in my hand, she says, the gold wedding band she has given me to distract me from my tears. It is there in the picture, although we can't see it clutched in my plump paw. It is our last unglimpsed knowledge of its where-abouts. I know it, feel it pressed into the soft folds of my skin. It brings the tentative smile to my face. The gold in my hand is the sun emerging from my clouded features. I am last to have it, the ring that binds my mother and my father, before I let it slip into the dense wild grasses.

PERSONAL

EFFECTS

The Budapest flat was long and sprawling. For a little one, it was endless. Along the floorboards worn so smooth I had only to watch out for the rugs with rough naps. If I slipped and slid on them, I'd get something red and sore. Some of the rugs were soft, though, and thin with age. They'd turn up and bunch and trip me if I wasn't careful. The rugs were islands with their own landmarks, like the raised bristly whorls at the centre of the one by the kitchen. I liked to sit on it in my warm felt pants and pat the horsehair surface gingerly. See how I could tame it? Along that brown river of a hallway, there were archipelagoes of throw-about worlds. I saw my mother take them and shake them and sometimes hang them out the window. She would try to rearrange them, but I made sure they found their right spots at last, the thick woolly tassels combed neat and flat.

The brown river parted for doorways, some always closed to me. "Karcsi's room. Stay out," said my mother, then to my sister: "Close Karcsi's door, before the baby finds his fiddle." And doors I wouldn't want to open, ever. The one with the great roaring thing that shook and rattled while it regurgitated water with a terrible rushing force.

On weekends Apu came home. His tread on the landing was our mother's cue to pull off her apron and tug her sweater smooth. There would be sweets if I foraged deep enough into the big coat's pockets. And the coarse rub of thick arms around me. Skin loose and tender as he held my face to his. I thought I smelled the animals on his coat. He talked about cattle, pigs, but it was just the soft musky fur of the coat's lining, sweetened by the smell of him. Karcsi would come out of his room to shake hands and would be asked to join us for dinner, although he ate with us most nights as part of his lodging, and his place was always set on the dining-room table.

We celebrated Christmas because everyone else did, and so we wouldn't seem too different being Jews. The big flat was surprisingly close with warm aromas and flickering lights. Evening lamps glowed. Up on the deep ledge above the dining-room door frame three small fir trees glistened with pink marzipan bells. I was allowed to finger them lightly when someone held me up. If it was a visitor, we were given a taste. The rough sugar coating grazed before it melted on my tongue. Pink, soundless bells, though their sugar, hard like crystal, made me imagine a little tinkling. I would gaze up from the floor, feeling sated.

The clapping made me startle. Who was this? Who was coming? The grown-up voices knowing and festive. Mikulás. Look. Look. Like a big brown bear. His great coat turned inside out to show the furry lining, and a white pillowcase over his shoulder. What? Who is it? Mikulás. Your Apuka. Look, silly, what is there in his sack?

My first memory was heat. I saw it. Waves of heat dancing. Later I imagined a small room with a black stove. I put red flames into the picture, flickering behind a grill. But I knew the image first through my pores. A pulsing reddish glow I ingested with each breath and sigh of my tiny, gorging body. The long rambling flat was difficult to heat during the coal shortage in 1954. Karcsi the boarder had a separate stove in his room, so that was the room my mother took for the new baby. Karcsi moved out onto the divan. At dawn he met the coal cars pulling into the freightyard and paid the black market prices my father had left him the money for, his fine musician's fingers gripping a sack of coal that by breakfast he let slide against the nursery furnace.

My sister came in to warm up. She stood first by the stove, and looked into the cradle at me. When my mother lay down to nurse me on the bed, my sister nestled her brief length along the curve of our mother's spine and took strands of our mother's long hair, twisting them around her finger. I felt heat, indistinguishable from the dance of gold shadows.

Out in the country on the state farms, my father trudged over crusty fields to inspect livestock. Wide hands thrust into the deep pockets of his heavy fur-lined coat, he spun dreams of spring crops and fall yields. Trusting implicitly that his family was safe and warm and unbeholden. How did he do that? Assume decency. My father anticipated decency in others before he would suspect anything else. Decency in others, even though he had had to leave his first wife and their child for a final labour service in 1944, and they disappeared with every other member of his family, in smoke. When I was born, Karcsi the lodger gave up his bed, and my father entrusted him with all that he had.

The shattering of glass behind us was a sound like day, clear and explosive. In the halls, apartment doors swung open, and from all of them people ran, spilling into the stairwell. My heart thrilled hopefully. Such excitement. With trembling fingers my mother buttoned up my little blue double-breasted coat, then I was swept up by Apu and tucked like a loaf under his arm. But I could walk as well as Lili, I protested, squirming. No time. My sister's able legs were a flick of white ankle socks in leather lace-ups as they flew away below me. I was bounced down the stairs urgently. My mother wore her warmest coat although we were inside. It flapped open as she hurried, suitcases in both hands. Sun poured down with us right to the basement.

Inside the basement was a camp. All the families from our apartment house were together. This was new and interesting. Bundles. Families spread on blankets. Food unwrapped, passed from hand to hand. From outside a deep rumble and vibration, distant and stirring. "Boom-boom!" I clapped gleefully. But my sister's hands covered her ears, and her face froze yellow as she hissed, "Shut up, idiot."

I learned a name for the camp-out in the basement. It was the Revolution. I tried the word in my head as my parents reassured Lili. Rev-o-lu-tion. There was fighting, but a revolution wasn't war, they explained. This revolution wasn't about Jews. War, Lili told me while our parents exchanged courtesies with the adults on the neighbouring mat, was when Jews were pulled from their homes and burned in ovens. This was only a revolution. Everyone in the tenement—Catholics, Jews, regular Hungarians called Communists—all of us there were equally at risk.

I took in the dim, densely bodied basement, learning and absorbing it like any new situation. It became part of me, the hours stretching into a predictable pattern of rhythms that I turned into the rituals of daytime and nighttime. The walk with my sister to the improvised bathroom. Threading our way past, and sometimes through, the personal effects of strangers. Habitual distrust in the glances cast at us, before they noticed we were children. Faces swerving at each unexpected noise, apprehension their common feature. I learned not to thrill so gladly to the drone of guns.

In the midmorning hush of a city that for days had been punctuated by bursts of shellfire and shattering glass, my father slipped away from us, out through a slice of light admitted by the basement entrance. They went out that day for the first time, men mostly, escaping tentatively through the fragment of light to forage a few facts that might let us know what was going on. No one was certain of the enemy. Hungarian troops were familiar but—Apu lowered his voice thinking Lili and I weren't listening—the Hungarians had in their ranks some of the old Arrow Cross members who had murdered Jews in the

war. And the Russians were so touchy they might mistake anyone for an insurgent. Russians were generally feared, it seemed.
But that day it was quiet, and the basement residents seemed to
tacitly agree that it might be safe enough to go out to investi-
gate. One after another, the men broke from their family groups.

It felt strange, the grown-up men gone. Almost like before,
when the men used to go to work. We were left as of old, the
children with the women, but my mother didn't appear her cus-
tomary certain self. She had held Apu back for a moment before
he left, as though changing her mind about letting him go. After
he was gone, she tried to pull herself together. "Come, Lili. Let's
make up the sleeping mats, then we will have a hand or two of
rummy if you still want to play cards." Lili dropped her book in
surprise at our mother's unusual proposal, for, even here in the
packed basement, our mother found countless chores to do.

When the door flung inwards throwing in the harsh daylight,
when the light burst in on us, it was as much an assault, that
brilliant flare, as the bereted silhouette that followed. He had
booted in the door, brandishing his rifle. The severe light
seemed to radiate from his khaki-clad figure. He waved his gun
at us as though we meant to hurt him. A sudden stillness seized
all of us in that basement. Lili's hand was a small sculpture with
cards fanned around it. We were still, as though not to alarm
him. Don't move. Careful. Don't scare the strange doggy. See
his sharp teeth.

"*Minden rendben van?*" Hungarian. Someone dared to answer,
so perhaps a Hungarian soldier was not so bad. "Yes," a woman
close to the door whispered, "yes, all right. Everything here is
fine." He tipped his beret, a peacetime courtesy, and, relieved
to withdraw without incident, backed out the door, his pointing rifle our last glimpse of him as it had been our first.

My mother's voice didn't lose its shrill fear, not even months
later when she drew on this incident during my parents' arguments and endless speculations. "When that soldier burst in and
we didn't know who or what he was, which would be better,
Hungarian or Russian, all we were aware of was the weapon he
carried, and our own pitiful dread." She wasn't going to cringe

like that again. Enough! "I saw Auschwitz, now this!" She wasn't going to raise her children in fear. "I've had enough cringing and hiding and hoping against the worst that always happens. I want something better to hope for. Milk the children can swallow without gagging." Voice rising: "I'm already thirty-seven years old . . . !"

When we finally emerged from the basement it was like blinking at a miracle. In my father's arms, ascending the stairs slowly, squinting into the light with every footfall. I entered our flat with the two men, my father and our tenant violinist. The windows splayed open. Before leaving the men had released the latches to minimize the impact of explosions. My father held me to keep me away from shards of broken glass. Wind gusted through the open windows. It seemed to me that the wind was sweeping in the very sky, there was so much cold light. It brought an emptiness into the unlived rooms. A purity. As if all had been wiped clean, sterilized by the light and blue air. Rooms that had lived something we had been spared—or denied; a life of their own. No longer the same rooms we had lived in. The men's voices boomed. The flat felt so empty. There were our things, the horsehair recamier and sturdy credenza, the framed photographs and fringed lampshades, even the throw rugs Apu stepped over as he hurried eagerly down the hall, checking everything. But they seemed insubstantial, almost transparent to me in that windy light. They had lost their solidity. Everything was light and airy as though even the thick oak table could be blown away in a breath of wind. The men's shoes resounded on the hardwood that skirted the carpets. It was as if we'd never lived there. As though in our absence someone had cleared out our personal claim to these belongings. Now there was only the idea of a sofa, the shadow of an armchair. All had filled with a light that was blue, clear, and so jagged it might slice you if you dared move. I flinched when my father laughed and our violinist put his head outside and waved. Human gestures seemed out of place to me, and risky, in that rare ether.

We were in a little car, hurtling past windbreaks on a highway. I was sandwiched between my sister and my father, conveyed into the countryside away from everything familiar. The sensation of being propelled against my will was as strange to me and as wild as I would find the ride, in years to come, in a Canadian amusement park, blasting around and around so fast my teeth were ground together. My mother's food packets were tucked inside my father's pockets. My mother had stood in her apron on the street, waving good-bye.

Apu liked to tell Lili stories about his life before the war on his family's country estate. Sometimes I caught references to the tobacco plantation and the horse-drawn carriages. When I heard him mention crop rotation, I imagined the fields spinning like the arms of the windmill in one of my picture books—one year up, one year down. Lili and I grew to imagine all that was good and beautiful to have risen out of his family's turf. The metre-long braided loaves of *challah* from my grandmother's kitchen, and tables set for twelve, sometimes twenty. Apu said his family had grown as rich and bountifully as the yields that fed and clothed them. They had lived on the land and nurtured it as lovingly as their offspring for three generations. These stories were part of the climate of our Budapest flat. Lili and I were accustomed to them. They had filtered into us like rain soaks a plant, and we understood that just as the seasons bloom and fade, so had my father's rural past.

Now he was taking us to the country. My father's fabled world was lost, but he was taking us nonetheless to see something he said was very special. Spring. Animal babies. Whizzing along in the little car, far from my mother and from Budapest, I wasn't sure what to expect.

Spring, ushered in by the rankness of wet winter rot, assailed us on arrival. The ground was mushy under our feet as though it would suck us in. The sodden fetid air we could only marvel at when our father said with relish, "Smell it? That is the earth blowing out its winter breath." Our offended urban nostrils flared in distaste. Feeling chilly in the damp air, we tramped along the muddy furrows. I looked to my sister for some cue, something to help me interpret the unpleasant sensations made more confusing by my father's obviously happy stride. Her boots seemed to sink into the furrows. Each step, as she pulled it up stickily, was laborious. She was ahead of me by six years. She was my measure, my yardstick. Hers the first impression.

"There was a calf born just this week," my father told us. "Isn't that lucky?" His voice sounded full with the pleasure of giving. But we weren't prepared for the dense stench of the barn and the rows of enormous beasts with their hot vaporous breaths. Lili had to be urged forward as Apu went down the row, patting the sides of the animals and pulling up their eyelids. I scrambled like a puppy beneath his feet. I was afraid to take a step away from him. I clung to his trousers until he had to pick me up. When he did, when I was up, oh, it was too late to look away. Something I wanted to hide from, but too riveting. One after the other he had pried open their eyes, checking for health. He had seen nothing to suggest disease. Not anything like what accosted us as a beast swung around presenting a back end that was red, so rawly red, every possible shade of red and plum unfolding like the layered petals of a giant bloom, all blood and flesh and tissue. A festering bovine backside from whose centre a black vermin seeped and crawled. I couldn't scream, lest putrid gore fill my mouth. Apu sucked back his breath in disbelief and turned, too late, to divert my gaze. My sister was already retching, a loud, raspy choke and surge.

As Apu held us in his arms outside the barn, trying to comfort us, he whispered into our hair and wept. He held us close, then wiped my sister's streaming nose with his monogrammed handkerchief. He stroked our soft hair, cradled our delicate bones, and whispered over our heads what sounded like a prayer, but was just the name of his other little daughter, the first one, our half-sister—lost in an Auschwitz oven. "Clárika," he kept reminding us. He remembered her in each caress he ever gave us; in each kiss on our foreheads and flip of a storybook page, she was always beside us, loved just the same. We were everything to him, I felt, but also we were never enough. As my father prayed over our heads his lost daughter's name, I imagined he saw the gulf between them stretch wider and wider.

Going home in the car, we didn't talk about the newborn calf we'd seen, or the baby chicks and new lambs. I played back the red gore of disease, and saw it mirrored in my poor father's dismay. He who had grown from the earth, who loved the smell of horseshit and fodder. I believed he could have grown a forest in a bed of salt, and in our Canadian garden he would grow a veritable arbour of fruit trees and flowering shrubs and beds that never wilted. How it broke him to see his children repelled so virulently by the living earth, and severed from the generations who had cultivated this land, loved it and nourished it and built from it a dynasty.

My family left Hungary in 1957. My mother retold the scene so often over the years, it acquired the quality of something tangible, like a family icon. My mother's hands had locked over those of her daughters, me on one side and Lili on the other. Her head turned to look over her shoulder at our father, who stood framed against the tenement. "With or without you," she said, putting argument and persuasion behind her. She led us down the front walk of the building, and said with finality, "We're going." My father stood rooted at the entrance. He was a man of European height, to become small only by North American proportions. His arms hung by his sides, and his face was carved in loss over loss. As he watched us, his face began to break down along these creases until it was the face I recognized later in galleries of modern art: the face of our century, its features skewed and misaligned. When he left the portal of that building his figure diminished with each step. By the time he reached us his shoulders had rounded, his chest sunk into his belly. He turned into the father of my childhood, the one I really knew. The man who never again trudged through fields of corn or patted the flanks of horses, who from that moment was always close by our sides, our Apu. A man for whom borders opened, but whose world shrank around the shoulders of his family.

THE
GREY
WORLD

CHANNEL
CROSSING

A small person in a kerchief on a jostling train, I hold fast to the windowsill as the train rocks me with its rhythm. I've absorbed the motion, so that after hours of gazing out the blurry window my own body sways and clacks at a mechanical rate. We're going. I don't dwell on the departure so much as our passage. Moving, going, on our way.

My father, beside me, has sunk into himself since we boarded in Budapest's Keleti Pályaudvar. I sense inertia gathering like a mass in his warm bulk. Occasionally a hand reaches out automatically to steady me, but my father doesn't seem to be moving like the rest of us; he's given himself over to conveyance.

Seated with us in the compartment, my mother rapidly reviews the names of those who came to see us off, remarking archly on absences. Where was Apu's colleague Mátyás? He couldn't wait to step into Apu's job with the ministry of agriculture, not even long enough to see him to the station? Old Agi's arthritic knees hadn't held her back from getting a good look at our relatives, although she had liked to complain piteously when she was mopping our floors. Poor thing, look at these biscuits Agi brought, dry as dust. My mother prattles while sorting the packets of foodstuffs that were pressed on her with embraces. She passes them along to Lili, who recites their labels in the fluting oratory style she learned at school. Lili's voice trills over cherry-filled bonbons. Apu lifts a hand, distractedly waving off my mother's chatter as though she misses the point entirely.

"Look, Apu, see the moo-cows?" I ask. But, although he pats my shoulder, I can tell he doesn't notice. Otherwise he'd identify their breed for me, sum up their condition in a glance.

The platform of the Keleti Pályaudvar had swarmed with our relatives and friends, most of them the post-war remains of Apu's large extended family. Blowing into his monogrammed handkerchief, he wouldn't look through the glass. His round face, at the best of times doleful, was shadowed under the brim of his fedora. His fleshy palm, my domain, failed to respond to my tugs: "Apu, A-pu, when will the train start?"

It vexes me when he drifts off into that other place from before the war, but he usually makes up for it, returning to me and Lili and placating us with a story he found there. I remember one of my favourites, starting like a once-upon-a-time:

"When I was a very little boy, just about your age, Danuska, not even four, I was taken for the first time to my beloved Great-Uncle Itzák's, to commemorate the *Yahrzeit* of his late father, your ancestor Hermann Grószmann. This was a grand occasion. Every year there came hundreds: relations, friends, rabbis, beggars from far and wide, for it was considered a blessing to give, especially to the poor. The more you would give in this world, the closer you would be to God in the next. And Great-Uncle Itzák was both a rich and a pious man.

"I was hardly more than a babe in arms, still with ringlets to my shoulders, but old enough to know that if I made a commotion my mother would not leave me behind. So, after a shameful display of willfulness that, I'm sorry to say, made my poor beloved father throw up his hands, he had the coachman put an extra fur rug into the *szánkó*, where, bundled in the back between my dear mother and father, I excitedly awaited the flick of the reins that would begin my first journey from the Rákóczi Tanya."

Who can resist the charm of horse-drawn sleighs and a father's childhood misbehaviour? But I resent it when he stays locked in that place and won't come out, assailed by other kinds of memories that make him feel no good can come of our endeavours.

I have no patience with Apu when he doesn't see that the bad things are over. Especially when it is daytime and he is with me and Lili. Things are good now, his children safe beside him. Not like the time when he was made to enlist in the labour battalion, board the train at their private platform on the Rákóczi Tanya, and be borne away from his family estate. Each labour service Apu went through, he's said, he thought would be the end of him. Yet it was he who survived, those he left at home lost. Vicious joke of fate, he has spat into the night. What kind of joke is that, I wondered. Wife, daughter, niece; parents, brothers; cousins, aunts, uncles. One night, in a fit of remorse-less self-punishment, I heard him count off the kinfolk lost. All hauled away by the rails he now presumes to ride into a better world.

Apu won't look at what he's leaving. The betraying grind of the wheels holds him fast. He can't accept he is abandoning all that remains of what he knew and loved. He is leaving yet again but—*by choice*—the dear familiar faces. He wouldn't look at them in the station despite my insistence on what was plain: "Apu, see. See! Blanka-néni's waving."

Apu does not glance out the train window as we pass the flat fields of the Hungarian countryside. He says no good-bye. From the first jolt of the train as it prepared to groan out of the Keleti Pályaudvar, Apu let go the reins. As the train jerked to a start, he disengaged.

Despite my father's withdrawal, I let myself be mesmerized by the flow of images on the window's changing screen. That Apu is gloomy does not really matter. Parents *are* gloomy. Gloomy and anxious and often irritable. It doesn't trouble me. I know

I'm central—Lili and I. We're a force that wrenches my father from the past he cherishes. We little girls, me trained to the window, Lili older but still charmed by store-bought packages, we small priestesses of motion are his transport. We were invoked by my mother for months. She wanted a future for her children. How was she to provide it when every penny he made he spent on his aunts and cousins? Did he not see while he fretted over the petty quarrels of the great-aunties that all his reaching into his pockets wouldn't recover their losses? She wasn't about to be sacrificed! Not she, nor anything of hers. His first wife and child went up in smoke. Enough sacrificed. Not her. Not hers.

Lili and me. Hers. Her children. It is spring of 1957. Gun-fire in Budapest during the fall revolution made her call up our names in the same breath as the future. We are going to a place where the future resides.

Apu pulls me down abruptly and holds me tight. He presses his face to mine, and his warm tears make our cheeks stick. It feels as though he's hanging on to me. Taken aback, I wonder with dawning alarm how I will manage to hold him up. My little arms wriggle and struggle free. They circle his neck like a life buoy, for I feel light and floatable and he is adrift.

Once we cross the Hungarian border there's no turning back. The passports, just exit visas really, only let us out. I deduce this from the way Apu concedes authority to my mother. In Hungary he was a patriarch to his family. He had a position of repute in his field. He was at home and in command of his milieu. On the train he can't even speak. Some internal inflexibility keeps him from testing new sounds. Apu lacks my mother's fluidity with language. She tries out foreign words on any train official who passes us. When she gets a response, however incomprehensible, her mouth sets in a satisfied line.

Lili's head rocks in my mother's lap. When I tear my eyes from the window, I glimpse Lili's big hair bow drooping atop her head like a giant butterfly with folded wings. I wish I could wear my hair like Lili's, but it is too fine to hold such an ornament.

Unlike Lili, I resist sleep and try to keep my eyes open. I think that by staying watchful I can prevent anything bad from taking place. Really I trust the worst is over, but it's smart to be prepared. If need be, Lili and I can benefit from the tragic mistakes of the past. We will know who to call, when to get out, where to run to, how to live.

Our half-sister, Clárika, as I've seen her in a photograph Apu keeps wrapped in his prayer shawl, was a serious child, bird-boned, with straight hair tied up in a fat ribbon like Lili's. But while Lili's mouth is full and usually animated, our half-sister looks pinched and studious, older than her six years. Beside her stands her cousin, who was raised with her on the Tanya. They look like mismatched twins. They're the same height, but the cousin's face is round and impish, with the same screwed-up little grin I wear in the passport photo taken before we left. It is the grin of the great-aunties and, Apu says, of his mother.

I don't imagine my grandmother with a screwed-up impish grin. I see her always on a death train, chanting a low prayer. She fingers something fine and beautiful as she prays. Mari-néni, one of the relatives who came back, said my grandmother was stopped before boarding the train by someone called Eichmann. There is always silence when that name is uttered. *Eichmann.* I cringe from whispering it even to myself.

"*Was ist das?*" Eichmann had demanded, holding up the white silk shawl my grandmother always wore on Yom Kippur. Mari-néni said my grandmother looked past the monster as though he were just a post and answered flatly, not in German, but in the Yiddish she knew he'd understand: "Clothes to die in." Mari-néni brought these words back to Apu like a keepsake.

She recalled too how my half-sister had held tightly to her mother's hand all that final journey. Her mother's gentle voice never faltered, calmly reassuring, "Soon we'll catch up with Apu. Soon we'll join your father." I imagine the pinched, serious child's face but can't hold it in my mind for long. It slides, instead, into the visage of the other, the little cousin with the wrinkle-nosed grin and abundant curls that might have saved the two children.

"The Rákóczi Tanya where I grew up was a big estate with many holds of land that we farmed for tobacco," Apu has told us. "It was the largest tobacco plantation in Hungary, but the estate itself was small compared to the lands next to ours, belonging to the Gyorgyi counts. On the counts' land there were two castles, no less. The eldest count, Count László, occupied the big *kastély* for part of the year, but no one in his family used the smaller manor house. The little kastély, as it happened, was located beside the Rákóczi Tanya, and one day, if you can believe, the count called for my father and offered to lease him the little kastély for our use. Jews in a kastély, can you imagine? Well, as it turned out, your beloved and devout grandmother could not. She told my father to graciously decline the offer. Appealing as it might have been for me and my young brothers to live in a castle, our mother would not dream of making a kosher household out of a place that had housed generations of Catholic aristocrats."

To pass up the chance of living in a castle, how I regret it! But my father sounded proud of his mother's response, as though she meant that the castle was not actually good enough for them.

Later Apu would have occasion to reject a proposal of the younger count's. Catching sight of the two little Jewish girls during the last months of the war, Count Ernö felt moved by the pretty cousin's typical Magyar beauty to make an offer. Let the girls come to him to be raised as his own. Come what may, he would do what he could for them.

Oh, I think hopefully, even though I know the real end of the story. I see that it doesn't have to end so badly after all. The children, the little children, as is right and proper and fair, at least the children could be saved!

"Let them go!" Apu wrote back to his wife in a letter from his last posting in the labour service. He was furious. What kind of proposal was Count Ernö making? How could the count allow himself to take advantage of the vulnerability of the children's mothers, while Apu and his brother Miki were away in service? It was a scandal, the very idea, to split up the family and abandon the children among strangers, *gentiles*. What assurances would there be for their safety? What was the matter with Miri? Was she so lacking in natural feeling that she could actually entertain such a notion? Under no circumstances should they let their child—or the other—go!

Not even one? I beg in my head, as I hear the bitter ending. Not even the pretty one with the impish grin? At least her, the one the count liked best?

According to Mari-néni, not once on the hellish journey had my half-sister's mother relinquished the little hand. Seared into mind as though I had seen them myself are mother and child, stripped naked, still clasped together under the spigots for gas.

The train, while it's moving, is safe, but when it stops I spin, panicked. I vibrate from the steel that whirs inside me. Though the train stops, I continue.

"Here we are!" declares my mother.

"What! Where are we going? What are you doing?" I gasp as she stuffs our scattered belongings into her satchel.

"It's Bécs, see, Wien—Vienna. We change here."

Change?

What change? Isn't it supposed to be days before we arrive at our destination? I can't stand being herded without explanation. I hate not knowing what to expect.

"Hurry," says my mother, bustling Lili into her overcoat.

There are so many bundles I can tell she'll forget something. Food, coats, blankets, papers. She seems distracted. Apu is already on the platform, weighed down by the brown metal trunk and our three leather valises. He is stuck with the valuables, the photographs of people I shall never meet, and all the crumpled, mud-stained letters he wrapped in a white, gold-threaded prayer shawl and packed away tenderly. We are supposed to have with us only what is most essential for travel, what we can actually carry, and he has brought the dead.

I am suddenly afraid for my father down there, separated from us and encumbered by that cargo. He can't forgive himself the harsh words he wrote to his wife. In punishment, I have heard him tell that story over and over again. I wish he would believe that it wasn't his fault. He had no choice when he was sent off in the labour battalion. And he couldn't have saved them anyway. He didn't know they would die. It was almost the end of the war. He has said himself that when he boarded the train for that last labour service, he felt as close to light of heart as the times permitted. The war was almost over. The Russians were outside their borders. So far, Hungary had escaped German occupation. But the Germans entered anyway and, in a flash, the person called Eichmann swept all the Jews out of the Hungarian countryside. Apu has said a number. Half a million Hungarian Jews gone in two weeks. That doesn't mean anything really, until I count his dear ones among them. How can he think that unforgivably, blindly, *he* was responsible?

I rehearse the list of our baggage obsessively, maddening my mother.

"Yes, yes. We have everything, don't worry."

But she doesn't pay enough attention, I think. She fails to catalogue what she stuffs away. Snatching up this or that and making it carelessly disappear. Someone must be vigilant, make sure nothing is left behind.

I can't digest what happened, that in a fleeting moment of time, everything was irrevocably lost. I struggle against that ephemeral instant, but it prevails. The brief but endless journey is my emotional locus, fixed. Apu's first wife and small daughter barely stepped into Auschwitz and were gone in a flash. Lili and I are so lucky. Lucky. Lucky. We were blessed with luck to have been born after all that.

"Apu," I shout, throwing myself from the narrow opening of the train, straight over the rattling steps into his quick arms.

Through Hungary and Austria, Germany and Belgium, the train has churned up the voices of conductors and vendors. My ears have turned numb to them, just mishmash and noise. I'm addled by what is new and strange. Landscape slides over my vision. As we cross Europe, past rivers, towns and forests, the landscape loses definition and form. It smudges together. The world whips by a blur of images that fuse, eventually, into universal grey. Days of locomotion smear the colours I have recently learned to name.

The train is my world now. The beat of its wheels has become my language, a restless tattoo I'm able to decode: slow screech of an approaching station; rattle of a trestle over a gully. Chugging is the song of speed. Like me, my father listens for its cues.

"Danuska, you hear? It sounds like we are stopping. Sári," he asks my mother crossly, "what's the next station?"

"How am I to know everything? You have the map."

But the map is in Hungarian, and the names not all the same as on the signposts.

"It doesn't matter, Danuska. We will get out and stretch our legs."

But I distrust stopovers. My heart beats too hard.

"Where's Lili? What's become of Apu?" I demand of my mother.

"He's just over there buying a paper. Don't worry."

"Where are our things? Why did we leave them on the train?"

"Don't worry, we're not staying here long."

"Where's the trunk?"

"Don't worry, we don't need it this minute. Here's Apu, are you happy now?"

Don't worry.

I long to be back on the rocking train, safe in the sounds I've grown to recognize, enclosed with my family and baggage in a contained compartment, safe inside while the wide world whirls past behind the transparent shield.

"Come!" I pull at my mother. "Come before the train leaves."

"I'll lose my wits if you don't leave me alone! See that conductor over there? Do you want me to ask him to put you on the train by yourself?"

The man in the uniform has heard and is turning to approach us. There is a light in my head, filling it up. So much light I can't really see. Now something floats above me. More brightness, but this time orange. Descending, the orange objects bring back to me what we have left: our circle of relatives and friends.

I recognize these things that seem to be beautifully defined by their finite orange shape. Extended to me from a precipitous height by the uniformed stranger, they look like golden orbs descending. Thick, pitted surface warming my small hands like suns. The fragrance is so sharp it rubs into my skin. When I pass one to Lili, the citric scent lingers on my fingers. Orange globes, tartly aromatic, juice-laden. I suck mine in, a draft of colour I retain long after the world outside washes grey.

The cloudy world mists over us, submerging us in the dull metal light of a northern climate. I succumb at last to a kind of sleep, falling into the grey world as into a waking dream, that swimming state you try to rise through, struggling for consciousness as for air. I don't actually see the waters of the channel. I don't remember crossing.

FLIGHT

The wet world receives us like a shipment of cargo. Like luggage, I feel flimsily held together by strings and brass clasps and leather straps. We're inadequately contained. My parents, so competent on home ground, have been reduced by the strangeness to uncertainty. Stunned and light-headed and tongue-tied, disoriented by the fumes and the noise and the volume of people, we're so clearly lost we must be shepherded from steward to porter to station attendant.

My mother's confusion rouses my father from the apathy he had felt on the train. She had been so eager to leave Hungary, so sure she was right. Now her bewilderment makes him feel needed. He gestures to passersby in Victoria Station. He holds out pieces of paper for them to read. Until now we've gotten by with some German, but my mother can't piece together the sounds she hears in London with the English words she studied in Budapest. My able parents are stripped of their natural authority. It frightens me that they don't know what to do or where to go, that we have stopped moving forward. There is a memory in my cells of a station platform where families are divided. It resonates through us all, underscoring our agitation.

Someone points us to a policeman in the station, but my parents instinctively recoil. Enforcement officials are suspect, even one unarmed and looking odd in a hat like a bell. Subtly my parents resist being led to an arm of any state. I see the reluctance in my father's thick inertia, an assumed denseness of what is being asked of him. The policeman in the pointy hat is their last resort.

My mother ventures first, her voice halting and high-pitched. The policeman touches her arm, and we tense. He lifts a finger —wait. Our eyes follow his few steps to a stall brimming with wrapped merchandise. As he adeptly picks out a bag, I'm charmed by the beauty of his easy knowledge. He tears open the top, proffers the bag first to my sister then to me, then kindly prods my mother towards a booth. I work the sweet brown glob in my mouth, observe him lift a handle inside the little cabin and pass it to my mother. He dials. In a moment we hear her rushing voice in our language. There are nods and smiles all around. My father pumps the policeman's hand; he thumps my father's back, and leaves us with the candy.

The policeman has left us the whole bag of candy, such beneficence when he probably has children of his own. I suppose that such a kindly man must have children. Lili holds the bag awkwardly. So much all at once. There is a message here, a promise I take to heart. All that candy for us, Lili and me. I love the sure swing of the policeman's long, black-clad legs as he walks away.

Lili and I know very well how the Jews of Europe died. Waking briefly from our heavy, child slumbers, we would hear the rising voice of our mother reliving its memories. Before we recognized all the words, we understood the sounds of grief. I'm under the impression I'm here to replace the dead children —my mother's niece, Dana, and my father's first daughter, whose name is my second one. Lili is called Liliana after both grandmothers. We learned our names through theirs, through their photographs and the stories told about them. We're the attempt at life out of the ashes.

Laci-bácsi, my mother's brother, got away to England before the labour service draft. He flew with the Royal Air Force and bombed strategic installations. Laci-bácsi free as a bird up in the air. I know how his parents and his sisters and their babies died while he flew above them, futilely flapping his wings. He will swoop down on us now, I hope, and whisk us to safety. He has made possible the papers and the passage.

We expect Laci-bácsi to meet us at London's Victoria Station, but instead a trim Briton recognizes the petrified family group huddled around its baggage. We are an island in the sea of Victoria Station, immobile as it washes around us. A neat, light-boned man breaks from the current. My mother looks up sharply and we raise our noses to sniff, sensitive as animals to familial spore. In his long, controlled face, witty eyes take in our discomposure. We're so obvious, it's amusing. He comes towards us with his eyes laughing and his arms unfurling from his sides.

Through his eyes I see we're comic. It makes my heart tighten even now. I resist thinking of us as lost, cast-up people. That it was me clinging to my father's trouser leg. I struggle against believing we were ever foreign and unfortunate. My life has poised on conviction in my well-being. I have calculated my risks against my good fortune to be alive, well endowed, well raised, well educated, well off. I have so rooted myself in this notion of privilege, I succeed in overlooking that I started off buffeted and tossed by the wind. Sealed in my car, I drive by bus stops where families wait in the heat or in the cold, their babies bundled against them. We were once there, subject to endless, degrading delays. I was there, and now I am here whizzing by. I feel a vast distance like a sea between the worlds we have inhabited in one form or another and between the different selves we've invented. My father was once a solid tree trunk with his back braced against the driving winter sleet, his coat open to shelter me. It's hard to accept that we were once so exposed to the elements.

My uncle, catching sight of us, can afford humour. We look so frightened when he knows there is no call to be. He knows where we are and that we're safe. He knows he has it worked out for us. This knowledge is in his manner, his amused expression and easy grace.

Washed up: we've been washed away from our bearings and swept onto a foreign shore. That this might be humorous tilts me off balance. It will be the central riddle of my childhood. I will grow to see my parents as besieged people performing on the essentially comic stage of a safe world.

My parents will build a satisfactory life. They will have a home and a garden and respectable work. They will raise and educate their children. They will have dinner guests *and enjoy them.* This is what my approaching uncle banks on. He doesn't expect to see the open graves of their hearts, but the possibility for renewal and pleasure. Renewal and pleasure and habitual pain will co-reside in my parents always. I will puzzle over the concurrence of these unmixable properties. They will cast in doubt the validity of my own petty trials. Against my parents' tragedies, my concerns will seem trivial; against the misery that befell them, my troubles will be mild.

As my parents hold their children and their belongings tightly in the human surf of Victoria Station, they cannot share my uncle's certainty that things will work out for the best. Nor will they share the confidence of their future neighbours in claiming contentment and stability. They won't be sure of their footing because the comic platform will never fully bear the weight of their pasts. This faulty equation will unsettle me. The vertiginous imbalance of then against now.

I see Laci-bácsi approach us in London's Victoria Station. We know it is Laci-bácsi by my mother's heightened alertness. He separates from the crowd, a small, graceful man, Laci-bácsi my mother's brother. When he greets us he is a pleasant Englishman who holds the future in his smile. "Call me Uncle Larry," he says, mock-seriously shaking my diminutive hand.

We had expected Laci-bácsi, the brother who schooled his younger sisters in off-colour ditties. We had expected a longer moustache, not one so carefully clipped.

I play my uncle's approach in my mind. The concise man breaking from the tide of station travellers. My uncle as he sees us bescarved and burdened with our metaphoric baggage. The little glint of humour in his eye. When do I notice he sheds something as he nears?

I see a small man emerge from the faceless sea that engulfs us. He is neat and sure and certain of where he is going. He is coming straight at us as if he knows who we are and what he can do for us. There is no trace of the central European about his tidy figure. His face is narrow, his nose straight. Somehow genetics have foretold his destination. Whatever past he brings with him through the tide of commuters, he discards at first sight of our huddled, fearful family. We are it, he has decided. We are the past, nothing fearsome, just typical greenhorn immigrants. I notice the lightening in his bearing, his jovial relief.

My mother will set him right, I'm sure. We love him in advance for his frailness and culpability. Poor Uncle Larry will have to pay for his failure to protect the lost ones. I see in his amusement what he doesn't know. When my mother and her sisters were forced to work in a German munitions factory, it was the bombs of the English that killed one of them. The bombs of the English exploding around them so that soil and sky were one burning mass, soil and sky and human flesh merged and melted and flying under the bombs of the English, the bombs of all that the English chose not to know.

Laci-bácsi comes smilingly towards us in Victoria Station. Finally we will be claimed. We will be plucked from the limbo of transit and identified again. We will have our names back, and our voices. But what he sees is not who we are. He remembers something else, has not accounted for a breach that is silent, pending and still as the air between a warplane and the ground. He thinks we're his past, but we are the remains. And *he* is not Laci-bácsi.

My overwrought mother falls into her brother's arms. We watch them embrace, the slim man and the lushly proportioned woman. She weeps. He holds her. He holds her tightly. We see that, how he holds her, all of her against his body. He holds onto her in this public place where we're growing aware this isn't done. People are looking. A reserved Englishman caught in a public display of emotion. The rhythm of her sobs enters him along his arms. We watch curiously as his hand creeps into her thick dark curls. He combs the locks searching, pulling.

"What have you done?" The Hungarian in his mouth is correct but rusty. "What have you done to it?" His hand tugs at the tendrils. "Why would you paint your blonde hair?"

They grew up together around the same mahogany table. They climbed the same tree, ran the same races in the fields. They pulled down their pants and thrust out their puny pelvises to prove who could pee the farthest. They shared a childhood but are so far apart this tidy man does not know, has not realized that her hair—because by the end the gassings were so hurried and so numerous they did not bother stenciling skin— the hair they'd shaved off is her tattoo.

My mother pulls away. We see she has stiffened with the other horrors he doesn't know. She touches his face. My father passes her his handkerchief. Finally she kisses Uncle Larry.

I feel indignant. Why is he spared what we small children were not? He is a grown-up, bigger and stronger and smarter. He should be made to know if we do. Uncle Larry's ignorance insulates him. If we don't tell him the truth, we will have to shield the English too, presumably, through our politeness and discretion, from their failure to protect the Jews of Europe. My mother musn't let Uncle Larry off scot-free.

She strokes the smooth face of her older brother, seeing in its vulnerability an obdurate denial of who and what has been lost. She has the power to change him. I wait for her justice. I expect it—the child who has been promised all that is good—I wait for a balancing, but my mother lets him go. She has opened her hands and released Uncle Larry like a bird. I see, as he shrugs his suit straight with a slight shudder, that the moment of danger for him has passed. Free again, he flutters aloft. We watch his wings catch the air and pull at it strongly. Uncle Larry beats hard, winging upward. Lili and my father lift in the current he has stirred. My mother's hands on my shoulders tug at me gently. We will fly across land, then above sea and over the hurdles of time.

RAIN

The pane in the leaded glass window whorls with fog and wet. Endlessly streaming rain distorts my sister's approach. She could be any of the girls on Monahan Avenue with bookbags on their backs and knees winking above wellingtons. Any of those similar shimmering shapes nearing our walk could be Lillian. But only one mounts the steps through the sloping rockery and comes into focus above the knotted tie, my sister Lili with eyes receding through round-rimmed spectacles.

Lili became Lillian when she started the first form in Purley. She wears a striped tie and a blazer with a crest that says Christ Church School. She was the first of us to become fluent in English. Along with her blazer and round-toed oxfords she donned British inflections and songs about Jesus. This doesn't worry our parents. War losses honed their Jewishness; Lillian's hymns are the least of it.

I wait for Lili in the long hour after infant-school. It seems to take forever. I blow on the glass, make trails with my fingers. In Hungary Lili was my companion. She sat and read me stories from picture books while Mummy queued up at the market for bread and eggs. I still look at those pictures sometimes, especially the one of the teddy bear under the green tree, with bright lightning snapping from a black thundercloud overhead. No one in the family reads me the Hungarian words here. I'm read to instead about a funny-looking boy called Noddy.

I don't want to play with anyone but Lili. The children at infant-school are as removed from me as adults. They're too fluent and adept at interpreting the codes of the English. I keep my mouth shut when I'm with them, to conceal my ignorance. But when Lili comes home I won't be alone any more. I peer into the mist at the hurrying older children, longing for my sister's arrival and the busy directives of her attention. But when she comes in dripping wet and dumping her bookbag on the rush mat, she pushes past me to the kitchen, breathlessly telling Mummy how Glenna left her at the corner and Richard Clark chased her all the way from there. I'm excited too by Richard Clark's interest and want to share in her conquest, but she's speaking too quickly while Mummy puts a pudding bowl in front of her, about strange names, times and arrangements I can't follow.

"Lili," I interrupt in Hungarian, "did Richard Clark catch you?"

"Can't she leave me alone! Can't I at least have friends to myself!"

What have I said to irk her so?

In the mornings, Lillian clutches my hand and walks me down Monahan Avenue. It's her job to take me to nursery since I made such a fuss when Mummy used to do it. We turn at the bottom of the street, then cross some corners. Christ Church School is nearby. Lillian doesn't have far to retrace her steps after dropping me off. Tugging my arm, she points with her other hand to the street she would take if she were walking straight to school. The morning light is dim, the air sodden. The street seems deserted as though we aren't supposed to be here. I'm afraid a figure might emerge from the mist, demand to know why we're walking the grey length of road without the accompanying authorization of an adult. The other little children arrive at school holding the hand of a grown-up lady.

When Lili prepares to leave me, I don't cry. I depend too much on her good opinion to subject her to that humiliation. I let her jerk the jacket off my stiff arms and lead me to a place at the low table. I keep my tears from welling by staring at the clock, not daring a glimpse at my sister's departing back.

In the big house called High Banks where Apu looks after the grounds, Lillian and I share a bedroom that feels cavernous. It has a high ceiling and what appears to me a vast expanse of floor between our two beds. When she turns and tosses, the wolf lopes over to rest his heavy paws on her sleeping form. His great pink tongue hangs from a panting maw, and long teeth frame a savage smile. I see him clearly, but am too frightened to move lest he lunge at me and breathe his moist meaty breath on my neck. My sister's stupid obliviousness is both reassuring and alarming. She's a perfect decoy, but what if the wolf eats her?

"Push off," she brushes past me in the morning when I try to warn her of the danger, "you're just dreaming."

Dreaming? Is everyone in this house senseless? This very morning the beast preceded us down the narrow winding stairs to the pantry. Its grey bristly coat and ragged tail slunk around the corner just ahead of my mother.

"Look, Mummy. The wolf. See before he gets away."

"Wolves now, in the house no less. Don't expect me to start setting a place at the table for it, too."

She is referring dismissively as usual to my friend George, who has become my constant companion.

"George doesn't eat peas, they make him throw up. Don't give us any peas. George says I wouldn't like them."

I don't see how anyone can eat peas as the English do. I watch how my sister tries to eat them the proper way, guiding them with her knife up the humped back of her fork. Usually they roll off and fall into her lap as she lifts the fork shakily to her lips. She works at this painstakingly. I'm doomed to fail before I try.

"I don't care if George doesn't eat anything! George is not you. The only George around here is the dog next door! So eat."

But the peas remain on my plate as they do on my imaginary friend's after I've cleared everything else off both.

"George says he won't go to bed until Lili does. He's a big boy. He can stay up as long as Lili."

"If I hear from George one more time today I will shut him in the larder!"

But George and I stay up and watch how Lili's hands are tied together to keep her from sucking her thumb and making all her teeth stick out. She succeeds in holding her book up regardless and continues to read while George and I drift off to sleep. I suck my thumb too, but not for much longer. George thinks it would be clever to drop the habit before Lili does. He insists that my hands get tied down too. Mummy and Apu are very pleased with me. They say I'm a big girl. What's all Lili's fuss? Her dark locks fall into her scowling face as she kicks the bedstead. George was right. I don't miss my thumb at all. George tells me how much nicer my teeth will look than Lili's.

Lillian was first among us to acquire the English language, but no sooner than she did, she retreated with it like a treasure she hoards between the covers of books. More often than not she's slumped over a novel in the half-dark of a room curtained to protect the furniture—or, I suspect, some secret she keeps to herself. Her absorption is infuriating. She locks me out of her world, shares none of its enticements. I run along the corridors of High Banks shouting, "Lili, where are you?"

"With her nose in a book, probably. Is it a wonder her eyes are weak, she doesn't get any exercise. Lili, can't you go out to play like a normal child!" Mummy shouts from the kitchen.

Listening to Mummy, you'd think Lillian wasn't normal. She needs spectacles for her eyes. She needs braces for her teeth.

She walks pigeon-toed and goes to the doctor to straighten her feet.

"Lili, come play ball with me!"

"That'll be the day, when your sister goes outside like a normal child."

I run through the big house, opening doors and calling, "Lili, telephone. Glenna wants you." The downstairs is still. The dining room and sitting room pose inert, as for a portrait. I race up the big staircase in the centre hall, pulling myself by the banister. "Lili, where are you?" She isn't in our bedroom nor our parents'. The other rooms aren't lived in. I throw open the doors on their awful emptiness. "Lili!" I feel stifled suddenly, breath stolen by her appalling absence. When I push open a remote door I see first the fangs. A frightful tawniness leaps at me, huge teeth bared, perpetually ferocious. My breath comes out in a scream. Lillian's head jerks around from where she's helping Mummy shake the dust from an old tiger rug.

"Serves you right for always following me around," she flings at my fleeing back.

Lillian and I leave High Banks one morning in the rain, keeping our heads down so it doesn't get into our hoods. "Hurry." Lillian pulls me. The puddles splash our knees. The drumming on the pavement picks up its rhythm. Rain seeps through my mackintosh, bats my face. Lillian trots faster, and I try to keep up. Soon the rain pelts us in earnest.

"Quick!" She drags me to a massive doorway, pushes me inside.

Out of breath. Gasping and gagging on the sudden dryness. So quiet, except for the rain thudding against the thick door and up on the roof, a quiet that feels foreign and off limits. The arched ceiling vaults above us, dark beams crisscrossing. A stuffy smell thick with chalk, dense and dry, clogs my nostrils. Air like heat that's too heavy to take in. My eyes light on something horrid, a twisted human shape hanging from its arms. There's no air here, so high and huge I'll smother. Scratching at the doors that won't yield to my measly weight. Starting a sound I don't realize is mine.

"Idiot!" Lillian thumps my shoulder, shoving me out of her school.

The grey stucco house looms behind me. I'm always conscious of its overbearing presence. I play on the stone slabs in the rockery, hopping from one to another. I know they're stone and grey, even when they're slippery with moss. I'm not fooled. Nor by the tinkly flowery bells that sometimes disguise them. Underneath, they wear the forbidding aspect of this place.

"Such a good child." My mother uses me as an example for Lillian. "She can play by herself for hours. She doesn't disturb anyone. Look how she tidies up after herself without being told. Lili, your little sister behaves like a woman already."

A tidy little woman, I wear my cardigan outdoors buttoned all the way down. I trail my hand along the fence separating the neighbour's property from High Banks. Behind it, the neighbour's blind dog snuffles and squirms its old black length trying to find me. I crouch on my side of the fence calling it by name.

"Here Georgie, here boy."

"Don't torture the beast," my mother half-heartedly chides. "He thinks you have food for him."

Georgie doesn't take walks with his owners. He's too fat. The best he can do is waddle once around the front lawn when he isn't too stiff. Monahan Avenue is very quiet before the older children come home from school. I whisper to Georgie through the wood slats.

"Here Georgie, hi Georgie." He noses towards me. I never touch him, but I can tell his coat is thick and soft. I wonder what it would be like to put my head on the warm furry pillow of his sighing belly. I talk to Georgie sometimes and listen for the quick pant of his response. I hope he doesn't eat so much he will burst, like my mother predicts. I would miss him.

ALLURES

OF

GRANDEUR

On weekends, we often ride into London at the top of the lurching double-decker to pay my uncle's family a visit. I like going back to the first house we'd entered when my family arrived in England. Three cousins had spilled from the front door as Laci-bácsi brought his little curved-back car to a stop. I stared out the oval window in the back. Boys. Much bigger than me, bigger even than my sister Lili. All limbs and knees. They pulled up short beside the postbox, quickly self-conscious. One of them slapped its tin side.

"Hi, no call for that!" Though I couldn't understand English I could tell from my uncle's voice that his reproach wasn't sharp. "Give us a hand then with the boot."

The boys, grateful for something to do, dragged our cases from the sloping trunk of the car. My sister Lili didn't seem to notice them. She ran her finger along some writing on the postbox, making out the letters. "Laurence W. Freed," she sounded out in Hungarian. "Is this you, Laci-bácsi?"

When we go into London for a visit, my mother always brings

along something warm and fragrant in a pan. Our cousins and their mum peer into the pan and sniff suspiciously, rejecting the delicacies my mother makes us on special occasions only. I feel offended on her behalf, but Mummy says never mind, the dish would be wasted on the English. Uncle Larry rubs his slim hands like a cricket and gives Lili and me a wink before taking a chair into their pantry. There he drops his carefully cultivated manner and gulps my mother's offering straight from the pan. On our way back to Purley, my father remarks indulgently that in the pantry Laci resembled his growing sons. Yes, Mummy says, satisfied with the success of her dish. With it she managed to reduce her flawlessly British brother—however fleetingly—to the greedy boy of their continental childhood.

My cousins aren't to know that we're Jewish, but we might let on with their mum. If we're at their house on Sunday, their mother pulls on her gloves pointedly, then herds them, scrubbed and grumbling, out to church. My uncle stays behind with us, but no one says anything for some moments after the door shuts behind them. We always refer to our cousins as "the boys," but in the wake of their departure we think of them as "his sons." *His*, but he lets them be raised in the faith of the oppressors.

Our Jewishness is best disguised. There was a time and a different place where being Jewish got you killed. That was before me and Lili; the world is better now. But on Friday evenings, my mother draws the drapes before she lights the Sabbath candles. The candelabra is what remains of two families' silver. It's been smuggled over many borders, sewn into a satin-covered eiderdown. On Fridays, Apu takes it from a drawer in the dining-room sideboard and lovingly scrapes off the waxy remains of the previous week's blessing. It *is* safer in England; in Hungary we didn't light candles at all. But my parents don't trust the tolerance of their Purley acquaintances.

We hide our Jewishness as a courtesy. We have no desire to offend those who have welcomed us. Colonel Reid from across the road, bringing a cutting from his garden, might be taken aback by the presumption of Hebrew candlesticks on a High Banks mantel. What might Lillian's friends from Christ Church

School make of Hebrew lettering on the spines of the prayer-books my father salvaged from the rubble of his birthplace, if we put them in plain view in the bookshelf?

On weekend walks along Purley's winding, hedge-lined roads, we sometimes stand in front of the school's double doors. "It's not really a church," Lili feels it necessary to remind us. Christ Church is a state-run school housed in what used to be a church building. Still, when we take in its arch and look up at the steeple, we can't help but wonder what we are doing here. How have we arrived at this?

High Banks, where we live, is the family home of Miss Tait. She is headmistress of the school where Uncle Larry teaches, and she shares a house nearer the school with her sister. She had asked Uncle Larry a lot of questions about the uprising in Hungary, her interest making it clear that it is decent to provide asylum for refugees of the revolution. Because she didn't ask about the war that had really changed everything, I presume it isn't as respectable to harbour Jews. Miss Tait has lent us the house with an open heart, but if she were to find out we are Jewish, it would reflect poorly on Uncle Larry. This doesn't make sense to me. The Golden Past Lili and I have heard about was distinguished by its Jewishness. All the cherished Lost World was by nature Jewish. Were my father asked what manner of person he is, he would answer "I am a Jew" before "I am a man."

Once in a rare while Miss Tait pays us a visit. She is my parents' most honoured guest, but really she is a nice English lady who pats my head and asks Lillian what she's been reading. She lets Apu lead her around the manicured flower beds.

"Mr. Weisz, you're a genius. Do you know how long it's been since the myrtle *bloomed?*"

My mother produces one continental delicacy after another from the dim kitchen where the table we children eat on has been dusted in flour for days.

"Surely you didn't make all this yourself, Mrs. Weisz!"

When Miss Tait leaves, my mother presses upon her packets of pastry to take back to her staff and to her sister.

"You're too good to me," Miss Tait sighs, as though defeated in the contest of kindnesses.

The big house in which we live is flanked by immaculately maintained properties. Miss Tait said Apu would be doing her a favour to pull the neglected grounds together, but we know it is really she who is magnanimous. On hearing that Uncle Larry's brother-in-law, recently fled from Hungary, was an agronomist by profession, she asked if he would do her the kindness of moving his family into High Banks and tending its garden.

"Garden!" gasped my mother when she first set eyes on the house. Looking up at High Banks from Monahan Avenue, I saw more windows than I could count.

Uncle Larry had planned a surprise. He had described the garden but deliberately didn't mention the house. The house and the genteel neighbourhood were his joke. My parents had arrived in England with just thirty British pounds, and within weeks they would be residents of a grand house in Purley. Enjoying his prank, and pleased with what he could furnish, Uncle Larry awaited their response. First my father nodded, as though in consent. Born into a wealthy family, Apu didn't take concerns about money too seriously. When money was a question, Apu would say with complete assurance, "Don't worry, God will provide." "God will provide," promised my father, who had been stripped by this same God of all he had held dear. "God will provide," he affirmed without a trace of sarcasm. He looked up at High Banks, then chuckled along with Uncle Larry. God had certainly provided.

I stared at the house, not catching the adults' humour. It was much bigger than Uncle Larry's, but, I thought, not as friendly. Grey, square, stolid, it overlooked Monahan Avenue impassively. Mummy's exclamation of surprise and Apu's delight in the rockery that ran down to the street didn't dispel my mistrust. Lili had bounded up the stone slabs to the thick door at the top. I gazed up at my big sister, who had receded with the height. Impatient to get in, she shuffled and scuffed her shoes on the doorstep. It disturbed me how diminished she looked up there, dwarfed by the house, her bare legs skinny beneath the pleats of her skirt. Small to begin with, I might disappear in the house's shadow.

"Aren't you coming?" Lili insisted. "Can't we go inside?"

It smelled chilly when we entered High Banks. Uncle Larry pulled open drapes as we passed into each room. The light made the dust dance, especially as he lifted the throws that protected the furniture. My mother ran her finger along the braided borders of chesterfields. My father kept one hand in his pocket, the other on my back urging me forward.

"See here, Dana," said Uncle Larry. "Shall we make the lady dance?"

The lady in a pink ball gown fit in his two hands. Something pretty shone in her dark hair. He held her up to the window, releasing the china's glow, and wound her at the bottom. When he placed her back on the small round table she twirled slowly to a tinkling waltz.

"How's that, then?"

I gave Uncle Larry my hand and let him show us the rest of the house.

Lili shouted, "Look at this, there are stairs behind the pantry!" Her shoes clicked her excitement over the parquet. I heard them clatter down the hall. Uncle Larry squeezed my hand reassuringly, but the house still seemed dark and cold, shrouded under cotton wraps as though guarded against our intrusion.

Mummy has taken on the house like an opponent. No one expects her to beat the years of disuse from its rooms, but she won't be outshone by the neighbours. She intends to make it clear that we are as good as the English. She and my father are well educated and well bred; she won't let it appear otherwise. She engages one room after another. Even those sealed and never used have their day in the sun when she opens their windows and beats out the dust. Urns and ornamental vases taller than I am are stripped of their thin cotton wraps. They look bland and shapeless until she unveils their exotic forms.

"For goodness' sakes!" she cries, rocking back onto her heels as though the colours on the vase were indecent. "Where did *this* come from?"

I ripple the lush silky fringes on lampshades never lighted, breathe their dust, stroke the plush insides of rolled-up rugs.

"Can't you stay out of my way? You're always under my feet!"

I'm intrigued by these collectibles that seem to have no real place in the lives of the English. Mummy speculates about them at times, but after wiping them clean, wraps them up without regret. No one feels any sentiment for these forgotten foreign objects.

"Allures of grandeur," Apu pronounces, poking his head in to see what Mummy has uncovered. I'm not sure what he means. "Allures of grandeur" is how he refers to the roots, position and wealth of his lost family. They had put their faith in "allures" when it is clear to us now that they should have given up all and run for their lives.

"Allures and folly," Apu sighs defeatedly before retreating to his garden. He makes it sound as if we were compelled to come to this place and succumb, as well, to the blandishment of "allures."

Grandeur notwithstanding, my parents work at a factory that makes televisions. I study the television at my uncle and auntie's. Auntie Christine is tall and slim with curls on top of her head. She speaks only English, unlike my mother who, in addition to Hungarian, can make herself understood in five other languages. Auntie Christine's English, however, has all the proper tones and glib expressions.

"A penny for your thoughts," she says, tweaking my ear as I gaze at the dead screen in the sitting room at their house. Rarely is it animated. It sits there, a dumb fixture with a doily under its two-pronged antenna. The speaker is covered in a textured crisscross design. I run my finger over the brushlike velvet and think no wonder the sound comes out fuzzy. The television cabinet is as sturdy as a chest of drawers. I can see how heavy it would be to load into a delivery van. My father is not a young man, nor brawny. He is round and soft with a head that is in all ways his largest part.

"Do you want it on then?" asks my auntie. "There's nothing to see until teatime."

On a couple of evenings each week, Uncle Larry teaches my father English by telephone. Apu struggles with the words in the newspaper. He sits at a little tiered corner stand, the *Times* spilling awkwardly from his lap, while Lili does her schoolwork at the dining-room table. I assume he chooses the small stand because he typically allows his children the biggest and best. He takes the smaller table, not because it happens to be the one on which the telephone rests but because of the kind of father he is and how we figure in his life. I imagine Uncle Larry comfortable in his sitting room, one light leg swaying casually over the other as he listens to my father read the headlines haltingly. Apu traces the lines of newsprint with one hand and holds the voice of Uncle Larry in the other. He declaims each word of world news laboriously, ensuing with a stream of commentary in Hungarian. He and Uncle Larry spend a half hour this way, mutually edified.

Uncle Larry teaches Auntie Christine, too. My mother barely conceals her pleasure in Auntie Christine's trouble with her studies. Auntie Christine wears rings with fat twinkling stones my mother says are real, "God help poor Laci." Any mention of the real stones is followed by the epithet "God help poor Laci." But Uncle Larry is the one who does the helping from what I can see. He wants Auntie Christine to get her diploma so she can teach school. My mother, who was a teacher in Hungary, bitterly acknowledges that by the time Auntie Christine finally passes her exams, she will still be stuffing English televisions with tubes.

Auntie Christine fails, but not because she isn't smart. During the examination her breath comes out too fast and light and the words on the paper begin a Charleston. As she describes this condition to Mummy, she grabs me by the hand, kicks her long legs behind her and breezily glides us down the hall to the sitting room. Auntie Christine's rings sparkle merrily as she dances. I don't see why God shouldn't continue to help Uncle Larry buy them.

One Saturday, Auntie Christine drops by in the little car to take Lillian to the shops to buy Christmas gifts for her school chums. Mummy feels slighted. Lili hasn't said anything to her about shopping.

"If that's what she wants to spend her allowance on, it's her money," Mummy says. Lili winces, wishing Mummy wouldn't always sound so grudging.

"It's not the same having boys, you know," says Auntie Christine, trying to smooth things over. "Boys just come along because they want you to buy them something. Girls take pleasure in choosing. This will be a treat for me."

Mummy doesn't answer. In her opinion shopping is a sport of the recently elevated peasant class; people of quality don't need to show off money. She doesn't like Lili wasting her few pennies on the spoiled children of strangers.

"You're so lucky," continues Auntie Christine, finger-combing Lili's tresses. "Girls are much more fun to shop for and dress. Shall we find a velvet ribbon, Lillian, while we're at it? A nice wine red to go with your dark hair would be just the thing for the holidays."

Mummy pushes back her chair noisily from the kitchen table, where she's been peeling potatoes, and wipes her hands vigorously on her apron.

"Lili has plenty of ribbons from home, unused in her drawer, some of them silk." But velvet is what the English girls wear at Christmas; I can tell by the expectant look on Lili's face.

Later that evening, Mummy holds the wreath Auntie Christine bought at arm's length, like something smelly: "She thinks she may bring this thing into our home and tell us what we must do!"

Apu says, "What harm? A little decoration to make the neighbours happy? It's nothing." He's so rooted in himself such trivialities don't matter. He had assumed the role of master of High Banks with ease, but also humour. Noting the heavy brocades and sensitive chintzes and lion's-paw table legs, he jested, "You see, we cannot escape the allures of grandeur." For Apu the wreath isn't Christian or offensive, just another of God's little jokes he has to forbear.

Mummy doesn't get it. "It's not enough she made my brother's children into gentiles, now she wants ours too?"

What does Mummy mean? All Auntie Christine has promised is a real English Christmas. Her voice sounded rich with offering and self-importance: holly and fruitcake, minces, Christmas pudding. There will be a tree and, of course, presents. She gave me a wink before leaving: "Maybe even one for you, Dana." I look forward to Christmas crackers that pull apart with a bang.

Something besides the wreath is gnawing at my mother. She's been promoted at the factory. Lots of people without English work there. Mummy's English is good now, and in addition to her Hungarian, Czech and Russian, she picked up German and Polish in the concentration camp. She is moved into the office to translate letters. This is good as far as I can tell, better than fitting televisions. But Mummy is a teacher. The promotion is an insult. No matter how well she knows the language, her accent prevents her from teaching the children of the English.

Uncle Larry tutors children after school to earn more money. "Imagine, making a man work two jobs so you can wear sparkles in your ears!" In Hungary only gypsies pierced their ears. Mummy can't accept that Uncle Larry has so departed from his origins, even his prejudices have been affected. "What kind of people care more for stones than for the life of a man?"

Auntie Christine's efforts to make us welcome seem to me innocent enough. It is my mother who's ungracious. "She thinks she is better," Mummy scorns, "because of what she wears."

As the holidays approach, Lili makes it her job to guide me through the Christmas story. Inexplicably, it seems to me, I have been selected to play Mary in my infant-school play. I know what I am, a little Jewish girl, the child of survivors of the war. And I know who Mary was, the mother of Jesus, that other God who was just a person. And I know I am the wrong child for the role, in all of that school for children of privilege.

Lili tells me why I've been chosen for the lead. As Mary I have just to look holy, I don't have to speak. I won't stumble over English. I'm actually the perfect child for a part that is just a pose. At school I rarely move about. I have told Lili about the German shepherd that ranges freely through the playrooms. I stay glued in my seat, tracking its progress. If I act like a statue, perhaps the bristly beast, its long tongue hanging from a permanently open maw, will leave me alone. Lili says the teacher knows I can be counted on not to move in the live tableau of the crèche, while the rest of the class tells the story and sings carols behind me.

Lillian wants to help me by sharing what she knows. I'm her little sister after all, and our parents aren't equipped for this. She tells me the story she has heard at Christ Church School about the star and the shepherds and the family in flight. They were escaping, she says, like us. They wanted to go somewhere safe. She says it will help me understand what I'm doing up there.

It does not. I refuse to understand what I find indigestible. I don't know why my parents in that audience of families on stacking chairs wave at me with pride. I don't know why being mum and stupid with a veil on my head is considered an achievement. I don't understand how they can applaud me as the Mother of God when she means nothing to them and it is all a lie.

I harden with anger that cements my performance. The Mother of God is a stony little statue. A white sheet has been draped over me, held by a band across my forehead. An icy truth grips my heart, fat and crystal clear like one of Auntie Christine's rings. I can learn to be just like the British, or remain with the fancy urns locked away in High Banks.

On Christmas day the table at Auntie Christine's is extended to seat the two families. It's piled high with platters my cousins corral down at their end. There's laughter: "How is it the food always gravitates to the boys' end of the table?"

Aglow in a blue blaze, the Christmas pudding emits an aroma that is spicy and strange. A pale blue halo hovers over the dark mound. It looks ugly, yet burns in a heavenly colour like the sky. Auntie Christine presents it with pomp, like a birthday cake. A homely brown pile, mysterious, aflame.

"Try it," the cousins coax, giggling and elbowing each other. So dark and dense, smelling sweet and pungent. I find the candied fruit inside and chew the mass energetically. Sticky and glutinous and strange, but I eat almost anything. Sweetly hot and hard to work with my small jaws. Around me laughter tinkles like the pretty glasses.

Suddenly my eyes gush wet, and my mother is yelling.

"What! What have you done to yourself now!" Her alarm and anger, often one, throw her into panic. "What's the matter?"

I can't speak. The metallic jarring in my teeth has spread into my jaw.

"How much?" a cousin laughs. "Pull it out. Is it a shilling?"

"No, it looks like just a penny's worth," quips another.

My tongue curls away from the horrid metal taste.

"It's only the Christmas money," Auntie Christine reassures us.

Mummy refuses to understand. She demands an explanation. "What do you mean money? There are coins in the food? You have *put* money in the food! On purpose?"

My mother's indignation feels like a balm. The others have all laughed. She's standing beside the table, trembling. "It is amusing, yes, to break the teeth of a child?"

"Sarah, Sarah, it's nothing but a custom." Uncle Larry strokes her arm, gently tugging her back down.

But she pulls away and snaps at Uncle Larry in a way I have heard her speak only to us. "It is a fine tradition you have now, Laci, that laughs when a child is hurt."

Apu refills the glasses, pained that my mother can't control her wrath. These people have helped us. They are family, *her* family, all we have left. Lili, too, squirms in her chair, mortified by my mother's outburst. Mummy is ungrateful. She is unkind and ungenerous and grasping.

I open to my mother's anger as to the sun. I feel released, as if a gate has swung clear before me. Excavating the mess in my mouth, I admire the currency it has yielded. I feel rich and very full as though she has made me a present.

MONAHAN

AVENUE

The usual clouds hang above Monahan Avenue. My mother shuts the heavy door behind us and looks up to check for rain. It is typically chilly, the sky weighted with damp that hasn't yet materialized. Mummy takes my hand and leads me down the road. Under my cardigan I wear a new, crisp black overall with a little pink posy stitched on the bib. It's nice wearing something new, like on a special occasion, only this is different. We walk down to the bus stop, which means the hospital must be in London, or somewhere beyond my infant-school or the greengrocer's. My mother carries a small suitcase with some of my things. The houses descend like stairs to the bottom of the street. I feel them urging me downhill, saying, "Get along now, Dana. Out you go." Mummy says I'll be gone a few days.

My mother was gone a week when *she* disappeared into a hospital. It went so fast, like a holiday afternoon, not like a week at infant-school that yawns towards what feels like an ever-receding weekend. I trace the silky stitching of the posy on my pants' bib over and over as we walk down the road. Pink and delicate and pretty. I'm not sure why I'm going. I don't feel anything hurting me. My mother has explained that the operation must be done in a hospital, just like when she had her stones. My mother's stones came from eating good things like butter and cream. She wouldn't be so stupid as to eat stones, but she got them just the same. I don't feel what I imagine as the cold clammy weight of stones in my stomach. I have been caught scooping butter out of the dish on the kitchen table so many times it's now kept in the icebox, but I don't think my parents would actually send me away because of that.

"Just a few days," Mummy assures me, "and you'll be all better."

I can't shake the feeling that I've done something wrong. It must have something to do with what the nurse at my infant-school called Mummy in to talk about. The shame of it, having your mother called in, but no one ever accused me of anything. There was some talk about the way it's done here in England. Every child must have his tonsils taken out. But it's so vague and bleary. I don't know what tonsils are. Not like stones that you can see.

I have the sense of being deliberately kept in the dark. Maybe my mother thinks I will make less trouble if I don't know why I must be sent away. Certainly I would be less tractable if I knew that I would be in hospital for two whole weeks. *Two weeks*. What largesse on the part of the British. My mother is not in the habit of explaining things in detail. She assumes my sister and I are quick enough to pick up whatever we need to know. What we don't understand is probably best not clarified until we are ready to learn it for ourselves. She adheres to a method of child rearing that on the one hand treats us like miniature adults, and on the other trains us like a higher form of pet.

We walk slowly down Monahan Avenue. The houses tip me forward, but my heels dig back. My mother uncharacteristically slows down, matching her stride to mine. Usually she's in a hurry. At home, in her kitchen, I stand clear of my own accord.

Mummy doesn't take the time to warn me she's about to whisk a hot pan off the stove. She is quick, purposeful and sure in all her movements. When Apu stayed home during my mother's illness, he didn't take chances. Overly careful, he told me to back away when he stood the iron on its end so he could check the oven. I knew very well the iron was hot, but I liked my father's attentiveness.

It was like a holiday being alone with my father. He didn't make me go to infant-school every day or shoo me outside. Apu pushed the iron methodically back and forth, and talked to me softly about the old times on his family's estate. It reminded me of the way he used to talk to Lili back in Hungary when I was still hardly more than a baby. Finally I was old enough to receive the same attention. I liked the scorched smell of hot cotton more than the mustiness of wet wool. I liked the way he included me: what should we have for dinner, the casserole from Auntie or the dish brought by the mother of Lili's school friend? In Hungary my father never did chores since he was home only on weekends, more like a guest. He looked funny wearing Mummy's apron tied high over his middle, and the laundry stacked up beside him in little rolled logs to keep damp. Should we go meet Lili on her way home from school? he asked. All his suggestions were delightfully out of the norm.

As we walked hand-in-hand, Apu told me about that other world like a fairy land, so full of all that was good. His home before the war was called the Rákóczi Tanya. When he said the name it sounded big and important, like London or Budapest. Bigger—the centre of the universe. As a boy he had driven between family estates in carriages and sleighs pulled by matched pairs of horses, and he and his brothers were pampered with wet nurses, governesses, tutors and—this impressed me most vividly—teddy bears made from the winter fur of hares. The phrase "winter fur" suggested all that was splendidly old-fashioned and fine. By the time Lili met up with us he was launched into the description of a holiday feast. Did we know that at Passover sometimes more than thirty guests had gathered around his beloved mother's table?

Back in our dim kitchen, Apu passed the broom over the cold floor in systematic sweeps, still talking about the festive meals he had enjoyed, listing each dish served on silver platters embossed with the family initials. I pictured steaming aromas rising like vapours of love. The dank chill of our kitchen warmed with the melodious flow of his voice. The cold melted like stiff cloth under the kiss of his iron.

"What's happened?" Mummy asked when she returned home from the hospital. She sensed the different atmosphere right away, even as she pulled off her hat and gloves. It made me realize she'd lost nothing of her sternness, removed stones notwithstanding. Apu took her in his arms, but she was impatient to look things over. He managed to hold her just long enough to pass me a conspiratorial wink over her shoulder.

I'm not convinced that I really need an operation. I think instead that I am being sent to the hospital to learn a lesson. My mother had a scar to attest to why she had been away. I pestered her until she showed me the angry red line running up her belly. Like a thermometer, I thought, showing when she might boil over. The new overall feels stiff and scratchy on my legs, so I take comfort in the pink posy that is delicate and fine. I finger it as we go.

A nurse all starchy white takes us up to the ward. Instantly I recognize the two rows of beds facing each other, just like the picture in my *Madeline* storybook. Two rows of beds for children without parents. From each bed a child stares at me as I hold the hand of my mother. They may have no parents, but I do, and mine do not want me. They can see that I'm being rejected.

"We're all full up this week," says the nurse. "It'll be the crib for you, love. You'll fit yet."

Crib. This is sheer humiliation. Mortified, I whisper to my mother, "But I'm four and *a half.* That's just for *babies.*"

"Never mind," she answers loudly in Hungarian so everyone will hear that we're not like them, "you'll just be a few days. When you come home your throat will be all better."

I'm so ashamed in that room among strange children to be thrust in a crib, so humiliatingly set apart, that I don't notice what she says about a sore throat or coming home again.

My mother comes to see me every day. In between visits, the time stretches interminably. Painfully shy in my crib, I don't speak to anyone but the nurses. Since I am quiet and well behaved, I'm left mostly alone.

Mummy brings treats and books and reads to me each afternoon after her shift at the factory. One day she pulls from her satchel a beautiful surprise.

"Look what Lili sent you." Lili doesn't like toys. Her imagination quickens to words on a page. Since she learned to read English, books are her chief amusement. She has sent her best doll. I think no less of the gesture because she rarely plays with it. I'm still honoured to be entrusted with the doll's safekeeping.

"Lili can't come to see you because they don't let children who aren't sick into the hospital." This is another of the incomprehensible contradictions I have come to expect. I'm here all the time although I'm not sick, but my not-sick sister cannot come to visit even once.

"Lili says you may play with her doll while you're here, as long as you promise to look after it."

Oh, I will. I stroke the doll's coarse hair as though it were an angel's.

"And Apu sends his love."

It is my mother who visits me each day; why never Apu? She brings fruit and biscuits and storybooks. There is always a special tidbit from my father.

"Apu is very busy. The garden has to be tidied up after winter, and there isn't much time for that when he gets home from work. Look, he sent you a macaroon."

I assume that my father stays away on account of the unnamed offence by which I have obviously let him down. I feel responsible for his absence. But mostly I blame my mother for leaving me each day.

"Bad mother." I greet her with this charge when she comes

in the next afternoon. "You're a bad mother. Apu wouldn't leave me here. If he knew I didn't like it, he'd come and get me."

My mother's eyes narrow. "Oh yes, your precious father who can never do any wrong. You girls think he is so perfect. But your father is afraid. He is a coward, I tell you. Afraid to see his baby in a hospital. Do you think I like having to say good-bye to you day after day? You think this doesn't hurt me too? I do the hard part and he gets all the love!"

My breath is an intake so sharp I cannot use it. I want to leap at my mother and slap her harsh mouth.

"Afraid?" It has taken me a moment to locate the thought, but now it looms large and glaring. "Afraid of what?" Panicking, I demand, "What's going to happen?"

But my mother has decided it's best to put the outburst behind us. She pulls up a chair beside my bed, and opens the storybook. "Calm down," she says, "or the nurses will think we're fighting. Do you remember what happened to Noddy yesterday? Think. Who picked him up in the scooter? What colour was it? So, we will read a little more. Listen carefully, and I will give you a treat when we have finished."

I watch the children in the ward roll in and out on special beds. They sleep a lot when they come back. Then the nurse brings them ice cream. You don't get the ice cream until you've rolled away and returned. So I wait. I've figured out that in due course I will get to roll out and have ice cream too.

When I finally go it's like I'm dreaming. Awake, yet dreaming. Strange to be carried and conveyed like a thing. Not unpleasant, not having to propel yourself. Double doors swing out as I sail through. More double doors. Poof—they exhale softly behind me.

"Night-night, love," says a disembodied voice. Then it's too late to resist the mask that shuts me down.

Darkness grabs me like a pillow against which I struggle to breathe and wake. It must be night. This dawns on me briefly before the searing in my neck closes out further thought. I try to scream but can't. My mouth feels severed from my throat by piercing knives. I grope for the crib bars but they aren't there.

My hands open and close on nothing. I find nothing to grab onto. I can't locate my voice. I'd disappear into the black night, a free-floating pain, were it not for these knives in my throat that pin me to the mattress. The ice cream when it comes is cold and numbing. Sometimes it's pink, sometimes it's white. It hardly matters because it has no taste.

As my mother helps me dress, I'm surprised the overall still fits. It feels a long time ago that I wore it, when I was much smaller. I've changed since then. Monahan Avenue too has changed. It's a lot brighter. The street is bathed in sunlight, a bright uncommon English sunshine. The heat makes the uphill harder work. The cloth of my overall clings to my skin. I've taken my suitcase from Mummy and it bumps heavily against my leg. Inside, Lili's doll lies safely swaddled in my underclothes. I drag the bag up the steep hill but won't let my mother take it. It's my burden. It belongs to me.

I am very aware of how different the street seems. Everything looks clearer than before, and sharper. My gladness, too, is so acute it hurts. I'm so relieved to be forgiven and allowed another chance. The blackness came and swallowed me, but I was granted a reprieve. I don't know why I'm so lucky. I got close to the abyss, teetered over the blackness, but it only got a part of me. Unlike that other little girl, my half-sister, Apu's first daughter, who never came back from Auschwitz. I will have to stay sharp from now on so I can see what's coming.

When I get home I plan to strip off these hot, scratchy clothes, throw them away, these wretched, traitorous pants that presume I will return the same as I went. I'm not that same baby. I hate any part of her trusting innocence. I itch to tear the guileless posy off the infantile bib.

Then I forget. As soon as I step into the cool shade of the house and out of the pitiless light, insight evaporates. Apu enfolds me like something inestimably dear, and Lili pulls me into the sitting room that is arranged for a party. For *me*? Life is seductive, erasing what I've learned. I have already lost it, the horrible fact of my father's imperfect protection. I'm pulled excitedly to something set up in the bay window. Overwhelmed, giddy, I don't immediately recognize what it is. Something new, a pyramid of blue and red squares. I gaze a moment, then lift the top block off the pyramid, delighting in its solid, wooden heft. I close my hand around it, feel the smooth, curved edges, hard but not jagged, satisfyingly substantial. The block has weight and bearing.

It doesn't take me long to become an avid builder. I build houses, schools, hospitals. I build enclosed pastures and paddocks that surround fanciful edifices characterized by fairy-tale towers. The blocks are the last thing I let Mummy pack before our trans-Atlantic voyage, although she repeatedly threatens to leave them behind if I don't clear them out of her way.

But it's not until we move into our new suburban Montreal home that the blocks realize the potential I had sensed when I lifted the brick at the top of the pyramid. I start to build bridges. I build them over and over again, using red and blue pylons and a yardstick overtop. I build boats from blocks by taping on white paper sails. "This is the *Empress of Britain*," I say, "and this is the *Queen Elizabeth*." I sail fleets on the pale hardwood floorboards I call the Atlantic Ocean, and pass them under the measuring stick held up by red and blue cubes.

Apu sits nearby in the white-walled kitchen, writing letters. Our mail in Canada is exotic. It comes from Argentina and Australia, Hungary and Britain, Haifa, New York and Philadelphia. Apu is constant and loving, a devoted relation to whomever he has left. And, over the years, some relatives he had given up hope for are resurrected, as if from the dead. He corresponds with them all, discovering from someone recently exhumed that another cousin he'd left for dead has resurfaced in Boston or Sydney or Utica. He reads the letters of reunion he composes aloud to my mother before sticking on the stamp. I pile up my blocks again, this time as high as possible without their falling. The yardstick balances precariously on top, thinnest of planks to be thrown across the void.

THE

NEW

WORLD

LADIES'

WEAR

"*Tiens*," my aunt Cimi said, standing up from the shop's worn parquet where she'd been kneeling to tack up the hem of the prom dress Lillian was trying on. She brushed some stray threads from her own spruce, figure-hugging skirt, then stepped back to get a good look at Lillian.

"*Tu vois comme ça change tout? Maintenant t'es vraiment mignonne.*"

Lillian seemed to agree as she studied her reflection in the floor-length three-way mirror. She had assumed a straight-backed pose in the balletic fourth position and three trans-figured Lillians gazed back at her from different angles, all of them irritatingly pleased with themselves.

My cousin Simone and I had peeked from behind the service counter where we were playing cards, suffused in the hopeful fragrance of new fabric. It was a privilege to be admitted into the adult preserve of Cimi-néni's store in Montreal North. I had promised Mummy not to disgrace her.

"That one's the nicest," remarked Simone, but I shrugged

without interest. It would be ages before I could fit into anything Lillian got now. I had just grown into the English woollens Mummy had stored away for me. How I had coveted the red tartan dress and two-piece mauve costume with the pleated skirt that Lillian had worn on special occasions in London. I aspired to be like her, imagining the swing of fine pleats against my confident stride, but when Mummy brought out the garments for me last fall, limp and stale from storage, reeking of mothballs, they had failed to transform me into the competent older sister. The wool itched mercilessly. I was more used to the nylon we wore now in Canada. And the mauve skirt hung shapeless, all its perfect pleats crushed.

"Don't be so picky, Dana," Mummy had scolded. "These clothes were good enough for Lillian."

Mummy draped the matching cropped jacket of the prom gown over Lillian's bare shoulders. Now my sister looked like a powder-blue brocade obelisk, with a spike of luxuriant dark hair. Mummy and Cimi-néni exchanged a knowing glance over the top of Lillian's head.

"*Oui, c'est comme ça la vie! Les jeunes deviennent toujours plus belles, quand, nous-autres, nous prenons de l'âge.*"

Cimi-néni's family's French and our family's English reflected the linguistic polarities of the city, but just by coincidence. When Cimi-néni and Uncle André fled Hungary, they tried living in France first, much like we had initially emigrated to England. Our adopted languages were both lingua franca in Montreal, where my mother was starting to add French to her repertoire.

Mummy didn't take aging as philosophically as Cimi-néni's comment suggested. Age wasn't really a threat to Cimi-néni yet. Vibrant, petite, with a shapely athletic figure, Cimi-néni bounced from showroom to kitchen and back again, still looking fresh. Mummy's beauty, on the other hand, had grown overblown and blowzy, like a blossom about to drop its petals. She pulled Lillian's shoulder strap straight and pressed her lips together as though biting back her irritation with her sister. It was boring, watching them ogle Lillian.

"Come on." I pulled Simone back behind the counter, but I found I'd lost my taste for Crazy Eights. "That's okay," my cousin said, putting up with my mood.

My cousin's nickname at our house was the Best Girl in the World. This was so true neither Lillian nor I felt particularly put out by it. It bothered only Mummy.

"Ah," my father would say as Simone danced into our house when Uncle André relented, letting her stay for an overnight visit. My father dropped whatever he was doing and stood up, just as he would to greet an adult visitor. "Here comes the Best Girl in the World," he said, holding out his arms to her in delight.

Mummy told Apu not to be a fool, he'd make the child self-conscious, but Simone's smile readily excused what she understood to be hyperbole. Like Cimi-néni, Simone was pretty, unpretentious and obliging. There would have been no contest among us. Mummy envied Cimi-néni for her daughter's pliant will and even temper, in the same way that she resented Cimi-néni's wealth. Lillian was high-strung and unpredictable, while my flaws were flagrantly apparent: I was selfish, loud and talkative to start with. And, unfortunately, I looked like my father.

"Yes," sighed Mummy whenever this resemblance was remarked upon. She took it personally. After all, I could have had the neutral loveliness that ran in her family. Surely it was contrary-mindedness on my part to take on the pronounced Semitic features of my father's side, when their brains would have sufficed. My cousin Simone hadn't made the same hapless error. Simone managed to look like her bear of a father, but such a sweet, translucent and gracious version it wasn't necessary to forgive her for it.

"We can say hi to Tante Helène, if you want," she offered, knowing how I liked to poke about the stockroom.

Tante Helène was Mademoiselle Foissy to me, but her doting over Simone extended my way—la petite cousine—the few times I was in the shop. Compared to the neon-lit showroom, the back office was dark and close and secret. Boxes overflowed with white plastic hangers. Others held tissue paper that was piled and pressed so immaculately flat I longed to grab a bunch to crumple. But even Simone was forbidden to touch things back here. Dresses hung on racks, set aside for alterations or held on deposit, no longer Cimi-néni's and Uncle André's to pardon if you soiled them with a sticky finger. There were treasures, too: trims, buttons, samples and remnants. The clean chemistry of unused fabric was headier than in the shop. I loved the oddments, more fascinating to me as scraps than as ready-to-wear, for I was an ardent seamstress of clothes for my dolls. In the tiny office, Mademoiselle Foissy perched on a high wooden stool, filling in the ledger. She cocked her head at us, a frail woman with her glasses pushed down on her nose.

"Viens." She crooked her finger at us, slid off the stool and led us towards some samples. "Regardes ces boutons comme ils miroitent." She showed us a cardboard flat of gold-painted buttons with sparkling glass centres. Knowing of my penchant, she winked at me and cut off a set of four. "Gardes-les pour tes poupées."

"Et pour toi, ma belle." Mademoiselle Foissy patted Simone's blonde helmet and produced a square pelt of synthetic fur that was so soft and plush I ached to wrap it around the unyielding shoulders of my bride doll. Simone rubbed it against her cheek. She longed for a cat more than anything, but Uncle André said that the string of au pair girls who worked for them at home came fresh from the country where they were used to letting cats run wild. There would be fleas in the house, dead birds in the yard and run-over kittens. Cimi-néni told Mummy that Uncle André had had enough of animals before the war. He would never have mentioned his life in Hungary to his daughter.

"Comme un vrai minou, n'est-ce pas?" Mademoiselle Foissy whispered conspiratorily to Simone.

The back door to the parking lot opened, illuminating the dim interior briefly before filling with my burly uncle. We all felt a little abashed, caught fiddling with the merchandise.

"Mesdemoiselles!" he exclaimed, feigning pleasure. My unexpected appearance in his stockroom meant that my mother wasn't far behind, and it made Uncle André nervous whenever his sister-in-law's inherently Jewish presence loomed into his life, especially in public, where his Canadian associates and employees might, by an indiscreet "slip" of my mother's sharp tongue, catch on that we were Jewish.

"*Alors mes enfants, vous vous amusez bien?*" he asked, lifting an eyebrow at the treasures in our hands.

Adept at managing her father, Simone showed that she understood the gifts were really from him. "*Merci, Papa,*" she piped, "*c'est si doux.*" She stretched on tiptoe, clasped her golden arms around her father's neck, and rubbed the patch of cloth on his cheek to share her pleasure with him. Then she planted two kisses, one on each side of his prominent beak. Knowing what was good for me if I wanted to keep the buttons, I followed suit.

"Hi, Uncle André. Thanks," I mumbled, discharging the obligatory smack. With Lillian's prom dress at stake behind the door, my mother would expect me to do my part to humour Uncle André. "Hm," he responded, barely politely tapping my back.

Uncle André was right not to trust me, I suspected. I liked to talk too much. I talked to whoever or whatever was around. Alone, I often talked to my dolls or sang to myself all the thoughts that flitted through my head. I was careful not to reveal anything to Simone about being Jewish, but even I doubted I was always reliable.

We trailed my uncle into the shop where he took in the scene at a glance. Mademoiselle Simard up front assisting a customer, two women browsing through the carousel of sale items, a grubby-handed toddler grabbing at the garments from his stroller. Lillian in prom regalia as Cimi-néni, instead of seeing to the unattended browsers, pinned on a corsage to complete the effect.

"*Et voilà, il arrive justement.*" She rose as smoothly to her husband's unwelcome arrival as had Simone. These feminine wiles intrigued me. My mother always got what she wanted by force of will, but Cimi-néni and Simone finessed their way around my uncle. Cimi-néni had intended to give the dress to Lillian as a little gift Uncle André didn't have to know about; now she would use another tactic.

"André," she went on, "*regardes ta nièce comme elle est belle!*" Lillian shifted awkwardly in her saddle shoes, suddenly self-conscious under male scrutiny.

"*Naturellement,*" said Uncle André with a chivalrous nod at my mother who, I knew, wouldn't be taken in for a moment. "Lili," he said, "you're now ready for the big dance?"

"Our graduation present for Lili," Mummy put in quickly, lest there be any concern that she was taking hand-outs from my aunt.

"*Ben non,* I won't hear of it," said Uncle André. Obviously he liked what he saw of the obelisk. "This is a big event. One little dress is nothing. Cimi, didn't we just get a shipment of new summer stock?" he continued, warming to the role of bene-factor. "There were some nice pieces, I remember. Lili, what do you wear?" He sized her up appraisingly. "Certainly no bigger than a six."

Lillian, saddle shoes forgotten as she grasped the bounty that was about to descend on her, surprised me with an artfulness that had had few opportunities to express itself between essays, examinations and books. Launching fluently into school-learned French, she assured Uncle André that she didn't need or want any new summer clothes. After all, she'd just be lounging all summer, in the back yard.

What could she be thinking to look crosswise at such a gift horse? Mummy would wring her neck. But Mummy, when I glanced in her direction, looked strangely self-satisfied.

"You don't mean to hide her away!" Uncle André addressed his sister-in-law, who was for once blessedly speechless. "That's nonsense. We could use a lovely young girl right here in the shop." Lowering his voice, he added something unflattering about the *desmoiselles* Foissy and Simard. Knowing shrewdly when to efface herself, Mummy retreated to a corner armchair and watched, gratification deepening as the afternoon pro-gressed, as Lillian let Uncle André turn her into a mannequin.

Barefoot by now, she preened in one ensemble after another. "No, that is too yellow for your complexion," Uncle André declared, and she compliantly discarded that number in favour of another. Once in a while Lillian voiced a preference, but the power of veto was ceded to my uncle. After all, Lillian seemed to imply in her gestures, the pleasure should be foremost the giver's. I couldn't believe a grown-up would actually fall for it, but Uncle André became ever more expansive as my sister pirouetted in front of him.

No sooner than a dress was approved by my uncle, Cimi-néni hurriedly wrapped it, so he wouldn't see how much Lillian was accumulating. Box after box, Simone and I carried the new wardrobe out back, stacking up a load my mother would stash into the taxi that would be more than justified by this shower of fortune. Lillian's thanks were heartfelt. Gracefully dodging the big hook of our uncle's nose, Lillian kissed him on both sides and promised to appear at nine o'clock sharp on the first Monday after the close of school.

Uncle André was visibly pleased with Lillian, who had grown, in the few short years since our arrival, to be so appealing. He was glad to reward her for adapting so sensibly. But mostly he looked relieved. For all his apparent pleasure in the afternoon's proceedings, Uncle André had pulled out dress after dress as though to stave off the inevitable. He passed a handkerchief over his high brow before bending to kiss his sister-in-law good-bye. Mummy hadn't denounced him this time. Not yet. Not once in the long afternoon had she succumbed to a foreign phrase that might give us all up.

A

REASON

TO

BE

"Lili?" Mummy asked casually one evening during summer break. Lillian had sunk into the armchair and stretched, fanning her sore toes on the teak coffee table. A nylon sheen emanated from her limbs, and the new synthetic fabric of her blue shift from Uncle André's store hadn't wrinkled despite the hot bus ride home. Two oversized white buttons seemed to pin the dress to each damp shoulder. Mummy stood framed in the opening to the living room, brandishing a soup pot she swiped dry with hard, purposeful strokes.

"Do you think at McGill, there will be a B'nai B'rith group?"

Wary, Lillian pretended ignorance. "B'nai-*quoi?*" she demanded. She had just matriculated with a ninety in French oral and liked to show off the fact that she conversed daily with the French-Canadian customers she served in Cimi-néni and Uncle André's shop.

"Don't be smart," said Mummy in Hungarian. "The university isn't going to be like Mountview High. At McGill you will meet all sorts of suitable Jewish boys." This was the first we heard of the term that became Mummy's code word for Lillian's post-secondary education.

Apu would get home later than usual this evening because it was Friday. First he had to stop at a deli on St. Lawrence Boulevard, to choose a Shabbas challah and coiled poppyseed buns for the sabbath *brocha*. Mummy picked up crusty white bread and baguettes at La Savoreuse here in Ville d'Anjou, but real bread—challah, bagels, pumpernickels and ryes—couldn't be had in our suburb. I rode my bicycle desultorily up and down Boulevard de la Loire, weaving around the crescent across the street from our house. It was too hot to pedal in earnest. I was hungry and impatient for Apu to arrive.

Mummy had been preparing the meal, off and on, since morning. Out on her lawn chair under the filmy awning of a sapling willow, she'd snapped green beans for the evening's cold sour cream soup. At noon, she'd chopped cucumbers and onions for the salad that needed time to marinate and chill. Mummy grumbled about being overworked on her summer holiday, but her meals were inspired by memories of her own mother's kitchen where, although Rózsa the cook had held dominion, only my mother's Mamuka's hands ever shaped the feather-light dumplings that went into their Sabbath soup. As Mummy dipped a moist slice of veal into a dusting of flour, then soaked it in egg and dredged it slimily through bread crumbs she had crushed herself, her face rested into a look that approximated serenity.

Apu, too, contributed to our meals, and not just with the foodstuffs he picked up on St. Lawrence. He could turn an incident at the office into a slowly building drama, sustained through countless interruptions about what the rest of us had seen or heard at school or in the neighbourhood. Last night, Apu had put down his knife finally, and, looking up from his plate, which he had cleared with appetite while we hijacked the conversation, asked in a flat, reproachless tone that never failed to arouse our curiosity, "Does anyone want to know what Mrs. Black said when she came back from the stockroom, and discovered, as I knew she would all along, that indeed there were a hundred and thirty-eight lots of green shirts, as I said there would be, and not the one hundred and fifty Manny the salesman had promised to ship immediately to the buyer?" And yes, of course we all did, even Mummy, who couldn't help but slip in one more invective against the aptly named office manager who tried in vain but with mulish persistence to catch Apu out in a fault. We wanted to know, because, over three courses and despite our interjections, Apu had managed to draw out a drama that depended on this punch line.

"Mrs. Black came out of the stockroom, and I could see she wasn't happy. She stopped by my desk, and I waited, knowing she couldn't turn this against me as I had warned her three days ago that the shipment was short." Apu's thin mouth twitched mischievously while Mummy unleashed a tirade against that stuck-up harpy who, if she wasn't the sister-in-law of Mr. Bernstein the owner, would have nothing much—certainly not *looks*, Mummy's supreme dismissal—to crow about.

"If your mother has finished," Apu continued blandly, "I will tell you what Mrs. Black said. 'Mr. Weisz, this weekend Manny will have some sewing to do!'" Apu's dour face broke into a shy, puckish smile as he relished the joke of Manny the big shot bent over a Singer.

Finally, I saw my father round the corner from Yves Prévost. Even at a distance, Apu couldn't be mistaken for anyone else. He had an odd gait, leading with his head, a residual effect of his childhood illness. When he turned the corner onto de la Loire, my world of bungalows, carports and duplexes shrank, looking toylike and fake. And he was out of place, weighted by his fifty-seven years and the jacket and tie he wore even in this hot weather. Head foremost, Apu plodded single-mindedly down de la Loire, bent to the purpose of erasing the last bit of distance that kept him from his family. Watching him come down the street reminded me that the other suburban fathers didn't walk; they drove, instead, in long cars, bare elbows thrust from sports shirts and jutting out the window. I sped up to meet Apu, hoping my appearance in pedal pushers and runners and on a pair of wheels mitigated, in a small way, his dislocation.

When the Shabbas candles were lit, the blessings chanted over wine and bread, and the curtains drawn for privacy opened again to the summer light, we settled down to the full bowls of soup I carried teeteringly to the table. Mummy topped them up before anyone took a mouthful. Apu cleared his throat. Instead of beginning his story of the day, he addressed Lillian, who had changed into shorts and a halter top. She looked more herself now, a fifteen-year-old girl with a guarded sulk on her full-lipped mouth. Apu fixed his eyes on her from under his bushy, high-arched ancestral brows, and asked meaningfully, "Lili, why do you think each Shabbas we light the candles and say the brochas over the bread and wine as have our ancestors from generation to generation?"

"Now what?" Lillian bridled.

"Lilikém," Apu remonstrated matter-of-factly, "no need to be so edgy. I wish to point out only one thing. Hitler killed my family, your mother's family; he took six million Jewish people. He tried to wipe the Jews off the face of the earth. Do we continue to be Jewish, observe our traditions, raise our children in the faith of our ancestors? Or do we help finish what Hitler started?"

Lillian's chair slammed back into the wall as she jumped up from the table. Down the hall, her bedroom door echoed the bang.

"Na—that was good work," Mummy said drily. Clearly, she concluded, she had done better. At least she had managed to get in those key words, "suitable Jewish boys."

Uncle André had assumed, on meeting the train that had brought us to Montreal from the dockyards at Halifax five years previously, that Mummy and Apu would follow his example about how to make a successful start in Canada. When he and Cimi-néni took us from Windsor Station to their Mountview bungalow, we gazed at the walls of snow banked on the sides of the streets, and the stark, rectangular buildings and the sleek, stretched cars, the high arched lampposts, the puny trees, recognizing nothing. Where we had come from was the past. This was the landscape of the future.

Arguments had flared almost immediately in the modernly furnished house Cimi-néni and Uncle André had already paid off. A few weeks after our arrival, I walked in on what was already an ongoing debate interrupted only by the days between our visits. I had wandered upstairs from the basement where my sister and cousins were laughing at a program but I couldn't catch all the jokes. I heard Uncle André's nasal insistence, speaking a French-accented English to discourage my parents from reverting to Hungarian.

What good had it brought any of them being Jewish? Forget about Hitler; afterwards, too, Apu had had to change his Jewish name to protect himself from Stalin. Show him one time it had ever proved an advantage to be Jewish.

Apu looked at my uncle pityingly, but with sufferance. "Do you remember, Brother-in-law," he said in Hungarian because he wasn't easily diverted from his purpose, "what Abraham said to Lot: 'Let there be no strife between me and thee, for are we not brethren?' Let's do the same. If you take the left hand, I will go to the right; if you choose right, I will go to the left. 'Is not the whole land before us?'"

Uncle André snorted dismissively and leaned forward, hands on his knees, about to launch the next sally. He hated having the old scriptures thrown at him. He knew plenty of those too, but preferred new terms of reference.

Cimi-néni fluttered around the living room, not able to tolerate discord. She had expected a joyful reunion with her sister whom she hadn't seen since the end of the war, not such unreasonable resistance. In England, their brother Larry lived like a gentile too; Mummy and Apu should be used to it. So what if Cimi-néni and Uncle André had converted? It was a safeguard for the future.

"Gábor," she importuned, "think of *tes enfants*."

"Yes," said Apu weightily, "it is the children I am thinking of. The children of Abraham, Isaac and Jacob. It is because of the children that we are here."

Unable to sit down, Cim-néni brought more tea from the kitchen. Her hand shook as she sliced the nut-filled *baigli* she'd learned to make at her Mamuka's elbow, and the first slice crumbled.

"*Chic-alors*," she cursed.

Mummy took the knife from her sister and ran it under hot water. Then she turned a plate upside down and drew the blade zinging across the porcelain. She tested its sharpness with sang-froid, against her little finger. Then, back in the living room where stillness had lowered, she pierced the toasted flesh of the perfectly rolled pastry. The knife slit cleanly to the bottom. She handed a slice first to Uncle André and then to Apu.

"I have one sister," she said, her voice hard and sharp in her native tongue, brooking no more nonsense. "One sister left out of four. Call up the children for dessert."

Before Mummy got her job teaching for the public school system, she worked at a Jewish nursery school in the heart of what is now called the Plateau, but in 1959 was simply referred to as beside the Mountain or the Mount Royal area. The neighbourhood was working class, Jewish, as close as we got in Canada to a dense, ghetto-like atmosphere. Double- and triple-flatted walkups built in the last century leaned into each other across narrow, heavy-trafficked lanes.

Mummy hated it. It reminded her of Europe. She hadn't come all this way just to arrive into the same old smells, same old faces, same old reminders of disaster. But despite her aversion to the district, jobs for my parents were initially available in the Jewish community. Uncle André used his connections in the garment business to get Apu work on St. Lawrence Boulevard among the Jewish delis, clothiers and textile wholesalers. My uncle did this grudgingly. Apu was an agronomist. Uncle André would have been happier to help Apu find employment with a government agency. All my father had to do was brush up his English and learn a little French. But Apu was too rapt in testing his new-found wings of religious freedom to try. The openly Jewish trade on St. Lawrence Boulevard gave him the justification he needed for having left his homeland. The Jewish shop names—Schwartzes, Moishe's, Finkel's Hardware—

warmed him in a way he had missed from his brother-in-law's welcome. Uncle André shrugged when Apu told him that the modest position of bookkeeper at Bernstein Imports was good enough for an old immigrant. My uncle had discharged his obligation. If his brother-in-law was going to be such a big Jew, let him stew in it.

But Apu didn't stew; first, he revelled. He had not seen caftaned Jews on public streets since before the war. What had been expunged from Europe seemed to him restored on St. Lawrence. One evening Mummy tied a scarf under her chin, then smoothed her caramel-coloured gloves over her fingers. Apu fussed, still folding and refolding more to his satisfaction the prayer shawl he usually took out only on the High Holy Days.

"Are the children prepared?" he asked.

"Don't be absurd. What do you want from them, they're just children. No one said they had to become *rebetzin*. Let's just go if we're going."

The street felt different in the dark than it did in the mornings when I came to nursery school here with my mother. Cars were parked on both sides of the narrow road instead of tooting their horns up the middle, and the walkups formed two solid embankments. Jewish people hurried through the fall air, the women wearing what Cimi-néni would call "*un vrai chapeau*" and the men in dark suits and hats, and clutching silk or velvet pouches like the one Apu had finally folded his prayer shawl into, but which he had tucked out of sight into his trench coat so no one on the buses we had taken from the east end would see. The children skipped along beside their parents, in their hands little white flags with blue Stars of David.

"Hurry," said Apu, "the service will start when the first star comes out." Lili and I scuttled to keep up with him, my hand in his.

Behind us, dragging her heels, Mummy answered sourly, "Don't worry. We won't miss anything the children won't be thoroughly sick of by the end."

It wasn't her idea to come back here at nightfall, but Apu

had got it into his head that Lili and I could use a little *yidisch-keit*, and Simchas Torah was just the right holiday for our first exposure to real tradition; this service was more lively than most.

"Ya, ya, a lot of old men dancing around." Mummy didn't relish sitting up in the gallery with a bunch of strange bewigged women while Apu took us children into the men's section that would get all the action.

The Clark Street synagogue was a small dark box with narrow slits in its side filled with thick multicoloured glass. In the arch at the top of each slit was a white, six-pointed star. "A mausoleum," muttered Mummy before we went inside.

The crush of bodies was intense, hot and sudden. I didn't get a chance to say good-bye to Mummy; she was swallowed by the crowd. Lili clutched the back of my coat. A strange bearded man noticed my empty hand and gave me a flag. Turning around, I saw him push one at Lili too. Apu looked for a space on the pews, but Lili hung back, so we remained standing. So many people in such a small building. Such a tumult. Even when the praying started, people nudged past others who rocked back and forth on their heels. But it was a spectacle, all the flags and Torahs wrapped in silver, others in different-coloured silk—white, blue, gold. It was lovely. The old men carried the Torahs around the room, chanting and dancing like Mummy said, while we waved our flags.

"Why do we dance, Danuska, with the Torah? Why are we Jews so happy today?" quizzed Apu.

Who knew, and who cared? We Jews were so rarely glad. Wasn't that enough? I must have shrugged, because Apu persisted.

"*Why* is always important. There has to be a reason. *Why* is what matters," he instructed. "On this day four thousand years ago, God gave Moses the Tablets. The Ten Commandments we read now in the Torah."

But the gladness seemed to me to have as much to do with the waving flags, the flag of Israel, a nation, a joy that made old men make fools of themselves. The crowd jostled and pushed together more closely as the leaders of the service paraded around the room, holding high the beautiful Books of Moses. Apu picked me up so I could see better. He held me aloft, and I felt presented, too, like the silver-crowned Torahs.

"You couldn't pay me to go through that again," Mummy exploded when we met her outside. "I thought I would faint, the sweat of all those women's bodies. *Phuy.* I don't know what you were thinking of, Gábor. We came for *this*? In the second half of the twentieth century we want our children to be in the Dark Ages? I couldn't understand a word of that mumbo jumbo! And it wasn't sanitary. It didn't even feel respectable, all that rubbing against strangers! Phuy," she spewed as though cleaning her mouth.

Apu was silent. I pulled on his hand. "I liked it, Apu, especially the dancing."

"And you, Lilikém, what did you think?" he asked, brushing Lili's cheek with his finger.

Why should Lili's ballot decide the vote? I thought. Two to two was an even split. Just because I was younger shouldn't mean my opinion counted for less.

Lili didn't look at him directly. "Here, Dana, you want my flag?"

I was delighted. Mine had torn from too much flapping, but Lili's was still like new. Waving my fresh flag at Apu, I saw him tuck his shawl pouch back into the inside pocket under the lapels of his trench coat. Disappointed by his capitulation, I judged that it hadn't taken much to clip my father's wings.

Lillian came home in the dark fall evenings from the Redpath Library, sometimes on the same bus as Apu, and after supper she didn't come out of her room until after I'd gone to bed. There was a Latin requirement at McGill, but Latin hadn't been offered at Mountview High. The compulsory phys. ed. course included swimming. Lillian couldn't float. The sea of bodies at McGill threatened to engulf her. One or two of her old high school friends had gone on to university, but on the campus spread over downtown streets and a colony of buildings each the size of Mountview or larger, Lillian and her friends didn't catch sight of each other in passing. They met at prearranged times for lunch, then had to fend for themselves.

My sister's difficulties didn't touch me deeply. I believed she could manage anything, as she always had. Skipping grades. Hungarian, English, French, now Latin. She was so much older than me, so smart, and so ahead of her age, I was sure she could do anything. She was just fifteen, after all, when she started university. Repeatedly assuring us, our parents would say, "With your brains and opportunities, there is nothing you can't do." They made it sound easy. Of course, if your standard was being gassed, tortured or stripped of everything you held dear, the rest would seem a breeze.

Lillian's days were long. By the time she came home, I had already finished my homework. Stamping her feet outside the door, she let in a rush of cold autumn air when she shoved her overladen bookbag across the threshold. Red fingers tugged at the scarf knotted beneath her chin.

Hearing her at the door, Mummy called, "Did you go to the B'nai B'rith meeting today?" before Lillian had even unbuttoned her jacket.

"No time," Lillian muttered, heading to the bathroom. "Maybe next week."

"Next week?" protested Mummy, following her and talking through the closed door. "Next month, next year, will be too late. By then all the nice boys will be taken."

This recent obsession of my parents to throw Lillian together with boys, Jewish boys, wasn't consistent. Until now they had jealously guarded her from all social events. Lillian and I knew very well what we were, and she didn't need a Jewish boyfriend to prove it.

I was in grade five, a dull year enlivened by a few changes in routine, like the strange name of a new arrival—Samra—more exotic than Dana. But she was a quiet child. Her strangeness, ultimately, didn't rival mine. Her hand wasn't always waving to show off that she was different, or special, or that she knew more about the world than the provincial children in our suburb. I looked down on my classmates for having no grasp of geography or sense of the events that had shaped our era. I could rattle off the names of world leaders, and, because my older sister was an anglophile, recite the kings and queens of England like a creed. I read avidly about those who had been noteworthy and were dead. All the greats seemed to have come from Europe: Madame Curie, Anna Pavlova, Louis Pasteur, Beethoven.

Hymns each morning followed the national anthem. The singing held off tedium briefly. But by October they too grew stale, always the same ones: "Jesus Loves Me," "God Sees the Little Sparrow Fall," "Swing Low, Sweet Chariot." The slim green hymn book was replaced in late November by a red one. It felt like a blessed rain after drought. Christmas carols. Oh, why couldn't we have them all year? None of this conflicted with being Jewish. Hymns and carols were just songs, more interesting than what we sang in music class: "Home on the Range," and "Row, Row, Row Your Boat" in double and triple rounds as if once wasn't mind-numbing already. Being Jewish was hard, clear and private, although sometimes it rushed heart-poundingly to the surface.

"I can't be here for the test tomorrow. A Jewish holiday. I have to stay home."

Heads craning for a view of my face that was suddenly not commonplace but worth staring at. Flushing because the teacher didn't really get the message and I was going to have to pronounce the Hebrew words with the accent on the second syllable making it sound more foreign—Yom Kip-púr—because in Ville d'Anjou there were parents who ate kippers and otherwise someone was bound to hold his nose.

Donna Tait was Jehovah's Witness. She had to wait outside the door while we sang hymns. It was against her religion. I felt sorry for her standing out in the hall just like the kids who got punished. But it gave me an idea.

"I have to do a project about Jesus."

"So?" said Mummy. She had been teaching in my school since I was in grade two, and she made it her principle not to request favours on my behalf.

"I have to make it into a book and put in pictures."

"Good."

"What do you mean, good? It's about Jesus."

"So?"

"I shouldn't have to do that."

"You're too lazy, Dana. You know, that's what you are."

"But it's not my religion. It's *against* my religion," I corrected myself.

"I wish it were against your religion to have such a *mouth*."

The best change at school was when the Bible Ladies came. Assemblies were always a welcome distraction, but the Bible Ladies were genuinely entertaining. Two middle-aged ladies stepped on stage in grey flannel skirts and plain blouses buttoned to the chin. They were greeted with thunderous applause. They ducked back into the wings as though they'd forgotten something, then returned, each dragging an easel with a felt flipboard. Unlike the simple felt boards we had in class, the Bible Ladies' boards held a stack of colourful scenes. Each felt page flipped up to unveil a fresh felt picture beneath. There was always the hint of a story at the bottom of the pile, one that we would have to wait to hear at their next visit. Cheering echoed off the high gymnasium ceiling, until one Bible Lady sat down to the piano and thumped a few chords. The whole school broke into "The Wise Man Built His House upon the Rock." Why, I wondered, would anyone bother to do otherwise?

Their stories were about Jesus and the loaves and fishes, and Thomas the doubtful, and Jesus when he walked on lovely, light blue, rippling felt waves. There was one about the money-lenders. Moneylenders were Jews, I heard someone near me whisper. And that awful heart-pounding flush swept me up, and there I was in the great big gymnasium, in front of the whole school, the only one with my hand in the air.

"Jesus was a Jew too." My voice sounded too loud in the hush of hundreds of schoolmates. An uncomfortable pause as children squirmed on their bottoms, unsure what to make of this assertion.

The Bible Lady hardly missed a beat. "Of course he was, dear, but he was also the Son of God."

I sat down, not convinced that she had gotten my point. I was rock-certain of what was credible. If my poor schoolmates thought a man could really be a God, they lacked essential mastery over the evidence of their senses. Talk about building on shifting sand.

From my perspective—one row up from the teacher with the other officious girls currying her favour at the front of the class—my sister and I were solidly Jewish. Living in Ville d'Anjou had heightened our sense of uniqueness, as though our family were the only Jews left.

Before bed I poked my head into Lillian's room, dim except for the desk lamp shining on the deep black of her crown. "Night," she murmured without looking up, absorbed in effort to get through the day's assignments.

She managed what she had to, but the cashmere-clad girls at the McGill chapter of B'nai B'rith weren't part of the pre-scribed liberal arts curriculum. Mummy didn't want to believe that at B'nai B'rith Lillian didn't count as a Jew. These boys and girls, Lillian tried to explain, knew each other from high school, or elementary school, or Talmud Torah. They went to the same synagogue youth groups or had bumped into each other at bar mitzvahs of cousins or friends. They lived in Hampstead, Westmount, Côte St. Luc. They came from St. Laurent, Town of Mount Royal or Nôtre Dame de Grace, all municipalities west of St. Lawrence Boulevard. "Ville d'Anjou? Is that on the island?" they questioned dubiously. It was enough to make Lillian's second venture among them her last.

What exactly was a Jew? I caught Mummy off guard one afternoon while she was still resting after school before starting to make dinner.

"Don't ask stupid questions, Dana. It's bad luck to pretend you're an imbecile."

But I wouldn't try to ask Apu, because he'd get a hurt remote look that made me feel I'd failed him.

"Are Cimi-néni and Uncle André Jewish?"

"Why do you want to make trouble? You know what they are. They go to church on Sundays."

"But Cimi-néni's your sister. She was in Auschwitz too. You said so. And Uncle André's family was Chassidic." I snorted, although I knew I was moving onto a minefield. The thought of Uncle André, with his painterly, French-style beret, deriving from a clan of caftan-robed Chassids was more than ironic; it was hilarious. "What about them? Do they still count as Jews?"

"You are what you are. Hitler proved that. It didn't matter what you called yourself."

"But then what about my cousins? Simone and Gérald don't even know they're Jewish!"

"Don't be ridiculous, Dana, they've been baptized. Their parents are, God-forgive-me-from-having-to-say-so, Christian converts, just like their beloved Paul the Apostle as they keep telling me. How can the children be Jewish?"

"You tell me. Look who's asking stupid questions!"

Mummy laughed appreciatively. She didn't like my big mouth, but she couldn't resist the bald-faced truth adults had too many reasons to dance around.

"Don't you dare say anything to your cousins. You know Uncle André and Cimi-néni are crazy when it comes to this Jewish question. Just be happy *you* don't have to go pretending."

But for Lillian to fit in at B'nai B'rith, she'd have to pretend lots of things that she wasn't. She'd have to pretend that all her friends weren't gentile, that her relatives weren't Christians, that we didn't celebrate Christmas with them, and that we belonged to a synagogue. She'd have to pretend that she was Jewish in ways besides the single most important one by which history had defined her.

"Mummy, why do you want Lili to go to B'nai B'rith? She's not like those Jewish kids. She didn't grow up among Jews."

"And what do you call us, you little know-it-all? What do you call your family?"

The temple in Westmount suited Mummy and Lillian's taste for the vernacular. In the ultra-modern sanctuary, the light-

studded domed ceiling that resembled the night sky shed a soft
light over red plush seats that flipped up and down like the
seats at the new concert hall downtown where Mummy had
taken us to see the Bolshoi. Mummy and Lillian appreciated
the temple's choral music and its magnificent organ. Apu
mustn't have realized that the pipes zigzagging up, down and
over the ark housing the Torahs were anything other than a
modern design. When the first reverberating chord rocked the
air under the dome of the sanctuary, he started, jarred to the
nerve by a sound he had never before encountered in shul. And
then the leaders of the service mounted the dais, decked out
in prayer shawls, but heads naked in the Lord's Temple. Apu
was fully aware that this was a Reform congregation. Only a
few men in the aisles wore *kippahs*; Apu was the only man in
a formal hat. But he had not imagined that a rabbi of any Jewish school of worship would stand before an open ark without
a shred of covering for his head. As the rabbi began to intone
the words of the *Shm'a*, I happened to glance down at the old,
mud-stained prayerbook that Apu held in his hands. It had been
his father's, and Apu had salvaged it after the war from the
debris of his family's estate. The prayerbook shook, and the dark
hair on Apu's wrist stood on end.

"What a beautiful choir," Mummy exclaimed as we left the
temple that first night.

"Choir!" protested Apu. "Who ever heard of a choir in shul?
They don't know the difference between a synagogue and a
basilica."

"And you won't accept any change. For you everything has
to be just like it was or else it is worthless. But this synagogue
is beautiful. The music is beautiful. The rabbi speaks in a language we can all understand. But for you this isn't good enough
because you didn't do it this way when you were a boy on the
Rákóczi Tanya. Nothing, not even such a palace for God, is
good enough for you."

Apu sighed. Again, the new world had bested him. Not Reform
Jewry, nor even Mummy, but the adulterated North American
rendering of values he held dear. If this was Canadian Judaism,

and if it contented his womenfolk to sit through a service con-
ducted in English, he'd have to settle for what he could get.

But, as it turned out, I was the one who got the temple. It
hadn't occurred to me when we started going to the odd Shabbat service, nor when we attended at Purim, or, in the spring,
at Shavuoth, that I was going to have to take up a kind of
permanent residence in the beth Adonai.

At Shavuoth I had watched the temple's confirmation class
make its procession through the congregation. It was like a
wedding with seven or eight brides. The boys in their blue gowns
held little interest for me. It was the girls I studied, their long
hair swept back off their faces to reveal sweet, open grace. Heavy
locks fell forthrightly, gleaming, to shoulders. Smiles broke from
flawless, tooth-straightened mouths. Gold signet rings adorned
the fingers that guilelessly held their bouquets. The girls were
the incarnation of virginal charm. I doubted that I would
achieve this transformation from the smart-alecky little pest I
recognized as myself, never guessing that this was my parents'
very expectation.

The confirmation class moved down the sloping incline of
the sanctuary, not with pride exactly, and certainly not solemn.
They basked. They soaked up the admiration that hit them from
both sides of the aisle lined with their families. They descended
by twos, boy and girl, girl and boy, in a blue gown–white gown
alternating pattern splashed with the deep red of the roses the
girls gathered to their breasts. The boys' arms swung by their
sides. No one looked ahead. The confirmants focussed on their
families and the congregation, winking at younger siblings and
cousins, acknowledging generous grandparents with disarming
smiles, narrowing their eyes at parents as though they shared
an inside joke. I twisted in my seat to avoid their glances, conscious that our only extended family would never step into this
sanctuary, let alone fill up an aisle.

Lillian successfully completed her first year at McGill, ace-
ing Latin although her swim stroke still lagged. The following
September, to my surprise, found me on the bus every Saturday
bound for the temple's religious school. Two buses and an hour

and a half took me across town along Sherbrooke Street from
Ville d'Anjou to the temple in Westmount. Sherbrooke was an
endless strip of dark canvas the bus wove in and out of the dis-
parate strands of the city. By the time I reached the temple, I
felt dazed from displacement, but one point was clear. I owed
this journey to Lillian because, for the first time in her life, she
had failed. Not at university, but in the eyes of our parents. She
had failed to leap the social barrier into the McGill chapter of
B'nai B'rith, and Mummy and Apu weren't going to make that
mistake twice.

Within a few weeks, the teacher from temple called to speak
to my parents. I had stopped going to religious school. I had
missed two weeks.

Mummy took his side. "Dana, there has to be more than a
few bratty kids you don't like. What a pleasant young man this
teacher is. There's nothing wrong with him. See how he
bothers. It upsets him, your not going. He wants to know what's
the matter."

Apu looked downcast. "Already you knew your *aleph bet*," he
said ruefully.

Why didn't the teacher mind his own business? I had thought
I was shut of religious school, until he decided to call. It was
easy for him to show his sympathy now by approaching Mummy
and Apu. They didn't know what went on under his long nose,
and he wasn't going to tell them. I hadn't told them either.

The next time he called, he asked to talk to me.

"Dana," he said softly, "this is Mr. Sherman."

"Yes," I said, steeling myself against persuasion.

"We all miss you in class."

Who did he think he was kidding?

"*I* miss you in class. Now no one listens to what I'm saying."
He laughed encouragingly, so I could feel free to joke too.
"Dana, are you with me?"

"Yes."

"Have we done anything to offend you?"

Had they done anything to offend me? More like had they
done anything *not* to offend me. The children ignored me. They

shoved ahead of me in line. They made snarky comments on the pattern of the tights that had come in the last parcel from England. They mimicked me when I courteously answered the Hebrew teacher's questions. What a laugh. They offended everybody, as he well knew.

"Dana?"

"What?"

"Has anyone hurt you?"

What I had felt was something different. Getting hit when you least expected. Not so much pain, as the shock of it. This was a Jewish school. It wasn't like Ville d'Anjou, where I had to be on guard against slurs, jokes, misconceptions stemming from ignorance. These were Jewish children, and I had assumed a common ground. I knew that however different these children were from me on the surface, I was stuck with them. If the ocean liner started to list, we'd be forced into the same lifeboat. But they didn't get it.

One of the boys had brought in a magazine with an article that had more photographs than writing. It was called "Remembering—Twenty Years After." The class clustered around him to look at the pictures. I knew plenty enough not to look.

"Lampshades. That's what they did with the skin."

"Wow, look at this guy: 'Look ma, no hands.' It says they did experiments."

"They could gas a hundred at a time in one of those rooms."

"Cool."

"What do you mean cool, you idiot, it was an oven."

I sat numb and stunned, not even thinking to tell them to stop. How could they be so interested, so *detached*? How could they not *know*? Didn't every Jew in the world know in their blood that it could happen to them?

"Hey, Janet, how'd you like that hairdo? Just wire her up."

"They took little kids and smashed their brains out on walls."

"Nothing would come out of your head, stupid."

I went to the washroom and sat. I must have sat awhile, because the teacher sent Tracy Cooper to see if I was okay. When I came back they were reading out captions.

The teacher had no right to call our house after he had let
the deaths of Mummy and Apu's families be turned into an
amusement for ignorant Jewish children. He wanted to know
now what I felt? He was asking if anyone had hurt me?

I felt a very hot shame that I had to keep from my parents.
They had been violated again, but this time by next of kin in
the land that made them free to do so.

"Will you come then?" I heard him ask as though he were
repeating the question. "Will you give us another chance?"

I had done many things before now to please Mummy and
Apu, but always to humour them. When it came to appeasing
our parents, Lillian and I had a habit of rolling our eyes. Mummy
and Apu were comically out of step with the brash, smugly
assured world Lillian and I were daily growing more to be a part
of. They took offence easily at the gestures of their neighbours
and colleagues, mannerisms that were merely colloquial and not
meant to insult them. Lillian and I had taken to viewing our
parents ironically through the amused lenses of our adopted
country. I didn't feel so much like laughing right now.

With a sinking sensation, I hung up the phone.

Apu took the bus with me. He came along Sherbrooke as far as
St. Lawrence Boulevard where he worked half days on Saturday.
He read the *Gazette* on the Ville d'Anjou bus, but then he folded
it into his briefcase, and began, once we were settled comfort-
ably in a double seat on our course west, to talk. Over the length
of the religious school year, on those Saturday bus rides, he
painted a picture of his version of what it was to be a Jew.

I had always known about Apu's lost world. Year in and year
out he noted for us the birthdays of each loved one.

"Today your grandmother of sainted memory would have
turned seventy-one." How was I supposed to respond to this?
"That's nice"? Or "What a shame"?

"On this day in nineteen hundred and eight your uncle Bandi,
my beloved brother, was born." Did he expect me to feel something? I had never met this uncle outside of Apu's anecdotes.

"Today my little Clárika would be a woman of twenty-seven."

A woman of twenty-seven, yet I was eleven, almost twice the age my half-sister had been when she died in Auschwitz.

These would-have-been birthdays were as ungraspable in their own way as six million or infinity, but my father stubbornly fumbled at them. He showed us photographs, some sepia-toned, but not all. Most were black and white like ours. All the faces were familiar as though I too had known them in a previous existence.

But although I had heard anecdotes, seen photographs and picked up many references to the people and places Apu had loved dearly, he had never before recounted from the beginning the story of his truncated life. I didn't know if this was his express purpose on the Saturday bus rides, to prepare me for my religious education; perhaps finding himself alone with me for uninterrupted periods simply put him in a storytelling frame of mind, for he was by nature a raconteur. It was much later, after my head swam with images of a world that seemed superior in all ways to the one in which we lived, that it occurred to me my father wasn't as naive or as vulnerable as I had supposed. I guessed he had heard from the teacher at temple what had put me off, and, over the course of those Saturday mornings, formulated a response to my dilemma.

Apu started with legends about his ancestors in the early nineteenth century and then, in more detail, moved through the generations of growth and burgeoning until his own birth at the beginning of our era. Here the plots split, mutated, multiplied. Stories of influence, renown, wealth and affliction. It seemed unlikely there'd be enough weeks in the religious school year to get through them all. He drew a picture of a clan, familial but worldly, large enough to have included the devout and the emancipated, the orthodox as well as apostate, all of them unswervingly Jewish. In the centre was my father, the willful child, bold adolescent, brave young man, daring adult. Be as I once was, he wished to say, not the defeated immigrant you have known. I imagined table-wide loaves of love, a palpable yeasty fragrance, and ached for that certainty we had all lost, of belonging to a place and a people.

Once begun, the stories spilled from my father as though they were inscribed in an internal script that he had only to turn on and play. I succumbed to the melody of his voice, its modulated, well-formed sentences, the line of narrative illustrated with references to the Bible. His Hungarian was literary and I didn't catch all of it, but the formality of the language resounded in its rhythms, and the underlying sadness of the story, however lightly it began, created depth he didn't have to engineer. Each week he picked up from where he had left off, always at a new chapter that would unroll like a carpet runner, from beginning to end, by the time he had to get up to leave.

At St. Lawrence Apu pushed open the red swing door in the rear of the bus, and glanced back at me before disembarking. This was where his journey ended, from the grand estates of central, prewar Europe to working-class St. Lawrence, Montreal's great divide. He'd lacked the confidence to continue. English started here, shoddy at first—Sam's Shoe Repair, a sign read; another, even dingier, The Philatelist—then drew strength from cosmopolitan downtown to the affluence of Westmount. St. Lawrence Boulevard's seediness dismayed me. Apu deserved better. But so he believed of me. As the bus pulled from the curb, I looked out the streaked window. He had stopped to search for my face one more time before the bus lurched off. Through smears of city grime, I met my father's eye. Then he touched the brim of his hat to me, releasing me on my way.

The sound of my father's voice on those Saturday morning bus rides forged something permanent in me, only the lesser part of which was Jewish. Apu always regretted this as his failing. In his view, the lost beautiful world had derived its vitality from Jewish tradition. But the vision I formed of Apu's clannish, populous relations was of a singular inclusiveness. He lived each day by the same precept, one foot in the present, the other in the past, unable even now to let go anyone he had loved. It suggested to me how Apu was able to give up settling among the Jews in Montreal's west end in order to live side by side with his in-laws, Cimi-néni and Uncle André, albeit distinct from one another, intolerant of their differences, fractious, yet cleaving together, the bond of a shared past too rare to risk for principle.

The kind of Jew I wasn't to become might have withstood the stares of the other passengers on the crowded bus, who hung above us from the overhead rail. But I was acutely tuned to their distaste for the foreign, older man who spoke too loudly in an offensively strange tongue to a girl who was likely his granddaughter. The bus didn't exist for him; nor did its passengers populate his universe. There were just me and him and the people he had loved more than his life. It felt all wrong. The wrong place, too public for so personal an accounting. And too mean for sacred recollections under the smoky exhalations of strangers who were so removed from his experience they could have come from the moon, they had as little sense of his worth. I felt a collision, a hard unabsorbable impact between our location in lowly transit and the elevated world my father hoped to transport me back to. For that, he would have had to stand at a lectern or a pulpit, at least to have held forth from a winged armchair in his own domain; not here under stony stares that took his elegant language for an insult, nor when he let himself be disgorged onto the penny-grubbingness of St. Lawrence Boulevard.

None of that mattered to Apu. Where or when, it was all the same. Least of all did he care how he was perceived; that was my bone to worry. Apu was simply a tool, his function memory. Why else had the Lord spared him?

When he spoke on the Sherbrooke Street bus on those Saturday mornings, I would stare at my father's soft, broad hands folded over his briefcase. The case, a gun-metal colour, was made from a synthetic material that didn't bend or show internal pressures. Not that there was much pressing against the case from within. Its contents were always the same: the *Montreal Gazette*, a cream cheese on rye sandwich, two apples, and a package of chocolate-covered cream puffs Mummy took as a personal affront to her superior baking. I chose to think the war had not so much reduced but distilled my father to these painfully simple needs. His index finger tapped once or twice on the hard side of the briefcase as he made clear his meaning. It was a big-knuckled, stubby digit. Its nail was shallow, square, cut close and to a point. Large blue veins crossed the backs of his hands, highly arched with the flow of thick blood. I watched the veins rise and fall as he drummed his fingers. The blood coursed deliberately from one hand to the other. I knew he could have spilled that blood himself, without the help of Hitler—in grief, or rage, or self-loathing—and I believed in my father's mysterious capacity for love.

THE

MAKING

OF A

JEW

When we first came to Montreal, we lived on the middle floor of a three-storey apartment block in Ville St. Michel, a working-class neighbourhood in the east end. A school with an asphalt playground sprawled across the street. In the back, spiral fire escapes unwound into a gravel lot. It was an adjustment after the elegant house we had been loaned in England, with the huge garden my father had tended lovingly in exchange.

Apu liked to take us to the Botanical Gardens at the corner of Sherbrooke Street and Pie-IX. This was his favourite spot during our two years in Ville St. Michel, before he and Mummy had a garden. He would put me and Lillian onto the little cater-pillar-like train that circled the grounds. While we lurched past sculpted hedgerows, he and Mummy strolled among the roses and manicured beds.

I liked the little train with its linked open-air cars, and its red and white plastic streamers flapping in the tepid air we stirred. Lillian and I would swing past our parents, and I waved enthusiastically, exhilarated by the novel sensation of leaving them in our dust.

Lillian hated it. I didn't realize then that she was homesick for England. Something in her turned in the afternoon's heat. The Botanical Gardens stretched flat and endless, without modulation. The drone of traffic from the busy thoroughfares put a lie to humming birds and bees, and produced a smell of exhaust that wafted over the sun-bleached beds. If the gardens were supposed to pass for natural beauty, this place was a sorry substitute for the grand green world she had adopted across the ocean. She hated being here, especially with me attached to her like a boil.

I didn't take her distress seriously. I thought it must be wonderful to be my big, smart sister, authority on all subjects. In England she had taught me how to pronounce the words of the new language correctly. Now I wanted to absorb everything else she was learning, and pestered her relentlessly. What was her school like? Who were her friends? Whom did she like best, and why were they better? I wanted her to explain her classes, describe her teachers. Why did they teach this and not that?

"Why were you born?" she spat out, before regretting it.

The words didn't upset me. Words in our family were hurled about freely. But I was perplexed that she had brought up the topic.

"Lili, are you sure you don't *know?*"

"Not again."

"Lili?"

"Can't you leave me alone."

"But don't you *really* know why?"

"How many times do I have to keep telling you?" she sighed. "We were accidents, mistakes. Why won't you get that through your head?"

Mistakes? She couldn't have been further from the truth, but I hadn't found a way yet to convince her. The mistake came before us. Everything had gone terribly wrong because of the war. The world was tipped off balance by all our poor dead, who had made the terrible mistake of slipping off en masse and throwing everything out of kilter. We weren't the accident. We were here on purpose to put things Right. That's why Lillian was so smart, so accomplished, and why I had to live up to her example.

"That's not true, Lili."

"Grow up," she said, surprising me again, this time by swiping at her eyes.

I wished with all my heart that I could oblige her, but I was only six then, and Lillian as many years older than me. And she had been jumped two years further ahead at school. We couldn't have been playmates any more than I could ever hope to catch up to her. Once we moved to Ville d'Anjou, the suburbs, I resorted to my school friends, my dolls, my sewing and the books Lillian gave me. It was flattering that eventually she thought enough of my potential to become my intellectual coach, but the books she chose were often tiresome. As soon as I could read speedily, I preferred the Hardy Boys, but politely slogged through the British schoolgirl series that used to arrive for Lillian in the parcels from our relatives overseas: *The Secret of the Abbey, The Abbess's Foundlings, The Abbey Girls at School.* Lillian couldn't get over leaving England.

I was more in my element surrounded by fraying fabric scraps and spools of different-coloured thread, toiling over tiny, poorly cut vestments and jabbing my fingers with needles I tried to push through wads of wool. Sometimes, after arduous hours, I would have to discard the garment I had laboured into a mess.

"Put it away. Try it again tomorrow!" Mummy would yell from the kitchen on hearing my howls.

I shut my door and started over, unable to let it alone, much like Lillian couldn't stop plying me with books to alter my point of view. I put off reading her offerings until any further delay would have threatened the peace between us. Closing the cover after making it through to the end, I'd say to Mummy, "There. It's done. Two hundred and thirty-three pages."

"Was it a good book?"

"Two hundred and thirty-three pages."

"Here," Lillian said after her next visit to the library. She was obviously satisfied with herself for doing me this good turn. "This is great." She passed me a book called *Stormy Petrel.* "I can't believe I found it here. The book jacket is exactly the same as the one I read in Purley."

On the jacket, a seabird hovered in the foreground of a British coastal scene, the colours predictably bruised as I remembered the English sky. I couldn't understand why this one thing that was so obvious seemed to elude my knowledgeable sister: England had been temporary, on loan like the big house we had occupied. All that opulent stuff reminded Lillian of what had belonged to our parents' families but had vanished in the war, along with the aunts and uncles and grandparents we had never met. We weren't meant to get it back.

I looked forward to the parcels from England with excitement. My best dolls had come out of those trans-Atlantic boxes, their hair so dense and firmly packed I could comb it as much as I wanted without pulling out a thread. Lillian approached each package hesitantly, afraid that it would fail to return to her what she hoped for most, the smell and feel and comfort of what she'd loved. After four years, she savoured the last traces of her British accent, still lit up at any reminder of that weather-beaten isle.

Stormy Petrel. "Petrol? Are you sure it's the same book?" I asked skeptically, doubting the reliability of her memory. Even an English book wouldn't try to spin a yarn, I thought, out of gasoline. "How many pages?"

The boy who arrived at the Ville d'Anjou house to take my sister to their high school graduation prom was infamous among us as the barely audible mumble on the telephone.

I answered the phone the first time he called.

"Mm spk ln," I heard, barely distinguishing a human timbre.

"Pardon me?" I asked. Before the days of obscene phone calls, children were instructed to politely ask a muffled mumble on the line to repeat itself.

If anything, the voice receded. "Mm ln," it dropped to an expiring sigh.

"Who? You want to talk to who?" I shouted encouragement.

"Li ..." gasped the caller, and I could tell that was final.

"Oh! Lillian! *Lillian?*" Understanding flooded me with a wave of excitement. The garble on the line was a *boy.*

"Lili!" I called, dashing outside where Lillian was studying in the sun. "There's a boy on the phone! A boy! Lili, a boy wants to talk to you!"

"What?" said Mummy coming up from the basement, her arms laden with wet laundry to hang outside, but already alert to something afoot. "A what?"

The "what" was called Alan ("What do his parents do? Where do they come from? What does he want from you?" demanded Mummy, implying an ulterior motive), and it took two or three more calls before he managed to get out that he was asking her to the prom. We had heard mention of this name off and on during Lillian's three years at Mountview High. Alan Bradshaw of the math prize one year, the science prize another. Alan Bradshaw who had broken his nose while quarterbacking the one football game Lillian had been allowed to stay late after school to watch. "But now you see what goes on," clucked Apu, "a rough and brutal sport that's no place for decent girls."

Until now they had managed to keep Lillian away from school dances. She was too young, younger than the others. She might be taken advantage of, Apu added in a lower register, which so infuriated Lillian she flung down her napkin and left her supper uneaten on her plate. But a graduation prom in all reasonableness could not be avoided after Lillian had worked so hard to finish high school two years ahead of her age group. Was it really necessary, though, to go to this dance with a date? Laney Henderson's father would be happy, they were sure of it, to drive Laney and Lillian to the party and bring them home at a suitable hour. In the end, my parents grudgingly relented. The date would be allowed if the choked voice on the line made a fully corporeal appearance a half hour before departure so Mummy and Apu could get a good look at him, and, of course, if he promised to bring Lili home by midnight. Lillian's mouth opened in a reflex protest, then she thought better of it.

"Don't go calling him back right away," Mummy warned. "Keep him guessing until he's so worked up he calls himself."

Skilled, direct and proving to be wonderfully effective at interrogation, Mummy wasted no time during Alan's pre-prom interview to elicit some salient facts from his mumbled, mono-syllabic answers. Short as these were, Apu couldn't decipher anything the boy said. Alan aimed his few words at the floor, where they got lost under the busybody patter of my feet. But Mummy managed to extract a few nuggets she stored away to share with Apu later. The boy came from Montreal North. He was seventeen years old, the only son of a Canadian ser-viceman and his British war bride—"Like Christine," she explained after Alan had left, referring to her brother's wife in England.

How Auntie Christine qualified as a war bride wasn't alto-gether clear to me.

"Mummy, Auntie Christine is British, and she never moved away from England. Uncle Larry's the one who left Hungary and joined her. Wouldn't that make *him* a war *groom?*"

"Thank you, Miss Know-everything, for getting me off the track. You think your father and I don't remember plenty about these British types, hoity-toity, too good to lift a finger. Your Auntie Christine was nothing but an orphan, who knows what kind of people she came from, but she had to have a ring even on her pinky."

Alan had said his father was a draftsman; his mother stayed home. Mummy's supercilious utterance, "Hmph," expressed con-firmation of her suspicions. If Alan's family didn't have more money than we did—and why would they when Montreal North was no Shangri-la?—his mother must be pretentious and lazy.

Satisfied that she had gotten to the essence of his background, Mummy had let the boy get up. At his full height, Alan would have been tall, but because he hung his head so he wouldn't have to meet anyone's eye, you didn't get the effect of his real measure. Even from my low vantage point, looking up into his bashful face, I hadn't succeeded in making eye contact. Apu held out his hand to seal the masculine pact regarding Lillian's curfew, but the boy just eased his weight from one leg to the other. A few awkward moments passed before he realized what was expected of him. Then he extended his hand with snail-like reluctance towards Apu, glancing up briefly at the wall behind my father.

"Did you see that!" Apu spluttered after Lillian and her date were finally released. "The children here are not raised to shake a person's hand!"

Mummy and Apu never ceased being amazed and appalled by the social gracelessness of the Canadian children Lillian and I brought to the house. Children who didn't know better than to walk right in without wiping their feet or taking off their shoes. Children who didn't say hello when they met our parents, or worse still, good-bye and thank you when they left. Children who didn't always answer when they were spoken to or, when asked to dinner, never once offered to help clear the table. "What do you think?" Mummy would shrug, insulted by what she interpreted as a lack of respect. "How can you expect the children to behave politely if they haven't been properly raised?"

Proper upbringing was a cultural deficiency here in Canada. The adults were overly familiar, lapsing into the use of Mummy and Apu's first names before they were invited to do so. And the children were untutored in simple formal courtesies. Good rearing was an attribute of which Lillian and I felt more than well endowed.

It went without saying that the son of a draftsman from Montreal North wasn't Jewish. Montreal North was like a previous but tawdry incarnation of the east-end suburb where we now lived. Ville d'Anjou had siphoned the upwardly mobile from the communities of the east end with its promise of spaciousness. We would have been surprised to learn of any Jew but ourselves who lived east of Pie-IX Boulevard. But nothing in our household went without comment.

"What can you see in him?" Apu morosely pondered aloud. "Lili, a girl of your background. Your great-grandfather stood up before the aristocracy in Vienna to plead the cause of Jews to own land in its Hungarian dominion. A pious, orthodox Jew, but a man of the world. A girl who comes from such stock, what can you see in a backward boy who doesn't have the character to look a person in the eye? A boy who isn't Jewish!"

Mummy and Apu said it often, in fact, between themselves and in front of Lillian. "The boy Lili has fallen for isn't a Jew."

"Who says I've fallen!" Lillian fumed.

But it was obvious. After the prom the muffled voice called more frequently, and with increasing expectation of being understood.

In her final year at McGill Lillian was called in to see her thesis advisor. She came home in the evening, excited by the news. Snow glistened on the tips of her hat. That winter we wore fur hats that buckled under the chin and burst around our heads like soft, tentacled space helmets. We called them eskimo hats, but it was a year before the moon landing and perhaps the vogue was as much inspired by the space race as by our weather. My eskimo hat was fake fur, of a uniform length like a dense crew cut. But Lillian's was the real thing, long-haired raccoon that fanned bulbously around her face. Coming in from the outside, sparkling and bright with cold, her head glowed in the dark portal like a human Christmas ornament.

The hat was a gift from Alan Bradshaw. This was the third Christmas in a row that he had bought Lillian something Mummy prudishly and disapprovingly referred to as an intimate gift because Lillian would put it on her body. First he gave her a silver bracelet with engraved Siamese dancers and little dangling earrings that matched. Last year, a jet pendant. The fur hat was his most extravagant present so far. It was a declaration from a boy who was sparing with words.

Mummy and Apu didn't accept Alan into their lives, but they bore him like other Canadian tribulations. In the summers, he was allowed up for the weekends to the cabin we rented in the Laurentians. Mummy couldn't help but show off her cooking to a fresh, unjaded palate. She broke him in with a cold, dayglo-pink borscht that later even she admitted wasn't entirely fair to a beginner. Mutely brushing himself off, as it were, much as he would from a quarterback sack, Alan managed afterwards to gird himself for each new obstacle she set before him: stuffed peppers; goulash; chicken paprikás; palacintas; cold fruit soups (his favourite it turned out was the same as Lillian's, cherry); floating islands the Hungarians called "bird's milk," which would have daunted the uninitiated, but by now he was game; chestnut purée coiled like worms, and the same colour, into a hillock capped with whipped cream. He was a good eater, that much could be said for him. And it was saying something; it showed in more ways than the obvious that he had inherent good taste. What favour Alan hadn't been able to win with conversation, he tried to earn through appetite. Searching, despite their compunctions, for a common ground, Mummy and Apu admitted that the boy might have something to recommend him.

Lillian stamped the snow off her leather cossacks but brought the fresh blast of winter with her into the house. She went straight into the kitchen where she knew she'd find Mummy.

"Professor Dawes asked to see me," she exhaled, rubbing her hands in anticipation of the warming effect of good news. "He said he's putting my name forward as the history department's candidate for a scholarship!"

"Scholarship. What do you mean, scholarship?" Mummy sounded grouchy. "You will get your degree this year."

"A scholarship to go to graduate school," Lillian continued, not registering Mummy's irritation. "In the States. He says I should apply."

"What are you talking about, Lili?" Mummy burst out as though Lillian had made an embarassing blunder. "You're not a child any longer. Look at you, you're a woman. You can't play at being a schoolgirl forever."

When had the rules of the game changed? No one had told us. The best news Lillian and I brought our parents always had something to do with marks. It was the most valuable gift we could give them, as though high marks were a moral imperative. Now Lillian had hit the jackpot, just as Mummy rendered it worthless.

"I don't know what you think life is all about, Lili. What you need is a practical profession, make a little money so you can

settle down and raise a family. Graduate school in the United
States!" She made it sound indecent. Then she slipped in
lethally, "Think about Alan. You would go away and leave him
after leading him on all this time?"

The pelt hung from Lillian's hand, its wet fur spiked in startled clumps. "What do you care about Alan! You never wanted
me to go out with him. This isn't about Alan!"

The outside door slammed. Lillian had gone back into the
cold and dark. Looking out from the living-room window, I saw
her walk down our path and onto Boulevard de la Loire. She
went as far as the corner of Place Croissy and turned back, then
walked as far the other way. She paced halfway up and down
our street in each direction as though there were a wall on both
sides that prevented her from going farther. I left the window,
went into my room and closed the door behind me. If I were
my sister, I wouldn't want anyone staring at me when I had to
come back inside.

Levine's was a ladies' clothing boutique on downtown St. Cath-
erine Street. The telltale name on its awning and the Jewish
salesladies who commandeered its floor were an illumination
for Lillian. The store was openly Jewish, yet prospered. The
summer after graduating from McGill, Lillian came under the
influence of Levine's. They recognized a find when it presented
itself.

"Weisz—you're a Jewish girl? You can work the cash?" Here
was an educated Jewish girl who didn't consider herself above
selling clothes, and could speak French like a native Québé-
coise. "When can you start?"

It wasn't a liability at Levine's to be obviously Jewish in a
public place. Its staff lived among other Jews in the neigh-
bourhoods of the west end. They accepted Lillian at face value,
a Jew born of a Jewish mother and a Jewish father. So what if
she lived on the French-Canadian side of town? This alien con-
cept went straight to Lillian's head like wine in a teetotaler.

Lillian brought home stories all summer about Levine's.
Levine's kosher butchers, Levine's synagogues, Levine's Jewish

neighbours. Mummy and Apu were taken aback. Lillian had never shown any indication of interest in Jewish tradition. Her regard for these Jewish strangers was an unexpected boon they hadn't hoped for once Alan appeared on the scene, and for the first time in years, he was temporarily out of the picture.

The Levine ladies knew plenty of eligible Jewish boys. There were sons, nephews, cousins. They teased Lillian and *nuged*: "Try it, you might like it." She had heard the same line used on Alan as he stared at a plate of comestible art he would never on his own have associated with being edible.

Lillian bloomed. Her slim figure swelled under the attention. Giddily, she entertained the idea, but stopped short of actually going out with one of these boys. She and Alan had been going steady for over four years.

"Cheating, what cheating?" Mummy rationalized. "You're not God-forbid going to sleep with any of them. It's just a movie. You'd go to see a movie. You don't think Alan's going to go out to a movie once or twice while he's working in Ontario this summer? You think he's going to watch TV every night at his uncle's house?"

Lillian submitted. It would have been rude to rebuff the generous offers of Levine's. "All right," she warned, "but just this once."

Mummy couldn't get over the gift that had fallen out of the blue. Apu smugly chided her disbelief. "You see, if you have faith, God will provide." Mrs. Levine and her pink bouffant hair-do was an unlikely transfiguration even for the Lord, but Mummy was too pleased to bother to cut Apu's high-mindedness down to size.

"I'll just wear what I'd normally wear to the movies," Lillian shrugged off Mummy's wardrobe suggestions. "It's no big deal. And certainly no reason to get your hopes up."

But hopes were up, they were up very high, even Lillian's. She was infected by Mummy and Apu's rare good spirits. The atmosphere at home was uncharacteristically light. Mummy's feathers didn't ruffle when Apu brought home French pastry from La Savoureuse. Lillian looked from one to the other as the *mille-feuille* left crumbs in the corners of their mouths. They had so few pleasures, how could she deny them?

In the week before the date, Alan happened to call from Ontario. Apu tapped on his watch twice to remind Lillian it was long distance. Finally, he gestured questioningly with his hands, indicating she was making Alan spend more money than was seemly. Lillian had consulted with Laney by phone a number of times before the date, but hearing Alan's voice, audible and intelligible to her in a way that eluded the rest of us, must have made up her mind.

By the assigned day, Lillian had stopped eating. Mummy was uneasy. "You want to look like a skeleton? At the best of times your backside is no bigger than a pinhead. What's the matter with you?" she fretted. "This isn't a funeral."

At three o'clock that afternoon, Lillian called. Mummy's mouth pursed as she listened on the phone, and tight lines radiated from it, drawing her cheeks together. "So, if you're sick, come home. But if you're *love* sick," she said as though she had a bad taste in her mouth, "I can't help you." Lillian was sick. In the toilet in the back room at Levine's she had retched and heaved and brought up a thin, sour fluid.

"When it's your turn," said Mummy, spinning around at me accusingly as though I were Lillian's accomplice, "don't be so stupid."

I was angry at Lillian. I had been ever since she went away to teachers' college and left me alone with Mummy and Apu. She had abandoned me in a cell with my parents and I wouldn't forgive her. The curtains were drawn, closing out the light Lillian had brought in with the books she had pushed on me but for which I'd developed an appetite, just as she'd anticipated. Over time the Abbey Girls had given way to *Heidi*, then *Little Women*, and later *Jane Eyre* and *Emma*. Lillian was my torch. She lighted the way ahead. She brought the world into our hermetic household—young people, ideas exchanged at the university, books read, movies seen, opinions that drove our parents up the wall. The house was stiflingly quiet, except on weekends when she came home and quarrels flared. Lillian ignited when she crossed the threshold of the house, and it didn't take much of a spark from Mummy or Apu to fan her flames. The year before Lillian married, I no more existed for her than the clothes she'd left behind in her closet.

Her wedding took place in the rabbi's study, a room that had seemed large and imposing to Mummy and Apu when they visited the rabbi to negotiate the terms of a reduced-rate membership to the wealthy Reform congregation. Fifty guests had to cram inside. It seemed out of keeping for our family to have pulled in that many people—friends, colleagues, members of the family diaspora who had turned up over the years in Boston, Philadelphia and New York. Perhaps now Lillian would stop complaining about being lonely.

She entered through the ceiling-high door, and we squeezed against the walls so that, led by my parents, Lillian could pass through to the chupah that had been set up beside the rabbi's desk. Mummy and Apu at each elbow piloted her around the canopy as though she were blind.

Nothing, not even the dress fittings or the photographs taken before the wedding, prepared me for the sight of my sister in her wedding dress. All that white like a blizzard that obliterates landmarks. Lillian's face wiped out behind a fountain of gauze. I heard the voile of her train caress the rabbi's carpet, the swish of each step press the constricting silk of her gown. This was what she had wanted. It was what she had clamoured for. Insisted. What she had spent a year fighting about with Mummy and Apu whenever she came home from teachers' college. I was sick at the thought that she was going to bring her French, her Latin, her years of British history, all her precocious scholastic excellence to encircle a boy standing waiting under the chupah.

It scared me, the sight of my sister subsumed in that monolith of white froth. She had never played with dolls like I had. She had not fastened then refastened with cunning tiny gold clasps the filmy train of a bride doll's mantle. I was the one who had fashioned fantasies from bits of shiny taffeta my aunt in England had used to pad the parcels of our childhood, because Auntie Christine was something of a seamstress too. Small bundles of rolled textiles tied up with ribbon or lace were wedged between the real presents of books and dolls. Unravelling a strip of maroon velvet, I would pray I wouldn't waste it and hack it to shreds, but at least approximate the regal confection for which it was obviously intended. While I worked my pedestrian daydreams in tight, crooked stitches, I felt secure knowing that my sister had managed to escape to a higher cerebral plane where she would, in due course, lift me up to join her. That together we would rise above what my parents had been reduced to by history and circumstance, and regain the poise and mastery that was theirs before the war destroyed everything.

Alan gazed at the floor, as was still his wont. He had taken a Hebrew name in order to marry my sister—Abraham, the name of the first Jew, also in a manner of speaking a convert.

A

PROPERTY

OF

CHILDHOOD

My mother's kindergarten was the showcase of our school. It was palatial, the size of three regular classrooms. The longest wall was window and light. Below the windows, a two-tiered shelf ran its length, offering toys that were clean, unbroken and not missing any parts. A standard-sized door in the far wall led outside. Dwarfed by the room, it admitted a single parent at a time, who my mother made sure was quickly evicted. The kindergarten was her domain. It had a piano, and enough instruments in a capacious leather-lined case to supply an army band. At the annual teachers' convention, she skipped all the workshops but visited each display in the convention hall, order book in hand. My mother's kindergarten was a gallery. Two of the walls were papered floor to ceiling with her children's art. It spilled into the hallway outside, filled the display cabinets in the school's foyer. The consultant from the school board selected the finest pieces to decorate the halls in the board building downtown.

My mother couldn't help gloating as she told my father, "Gibbs he just sniffs. Mrs. Lenahan the consultant says—right in front of me—'Mrs. Weisz is a gem, Mr. Gibbs. She makes all of us shine.' That's why he sniffs. If I wasn't there, he would show off that he found me. Of course that isn't true. I asked for a school in our neighbourhood."

My mother was quick to feel slights. "That Pratt woman thinks she can frighten me because I am a foreigner? I told her my words are broken yes, but my eyes are good. I saw her boy smack the other, not just one time. And Gibbs he is standing there smiling in his moustache. He says, 'Mrs. Weisz runs a tight ship in the kindergarten.' But why is he smiling? He makes me look like a fool."

When the principal came into our classroom and we scraped briskly and obsequiously to our feet, I knew something the others didn't. I knew he couldn't be trusted.

"Good morning, boys and girls." Heat melted the back of my neck. Thirty wooden chairs scraped over linoleum. My mother had entered my classroom. Sly grins and sideways glances at me. Was I to lilt with the rest, "Good morning, Mrs. Weisz"? Mortifying to stand up for your own mother, but then it would be worse if you were the only one sitting down.

"The big snow today makes your teacher late. But we can sing some songs—yes?—to keep us warm, then we will do a little work. What do we sing first?"

Heads swerved around to see if my hand was up. My raised hand was a fixture in the classroom. My mother sang pleasantly. She played the piano in her kindergarten and she could be heard when you took a note to the office. Kids standing in front of the office for a minor offence grinned at me and mouthed the nursery song "A-B-C-D-E-F-G."

My mother's accent was painful because it made her appear vulnerable. When the other kids said, "You got all those Es on your report because your mother's a teacher," it wasn't about me; they were pointing at her difference. My mother prided herself on not interfering with my schooling. She was indignant about slurs. "You should have seen that Gibbs. Second year in a row the Jewish child gets the Excellents, and he can do nothing. But you think he would say to me even a little 'Congratulations'? He says to the Polish one, you know, Borkowski with the big house on Boisvert Street, how his Mandy was good." What pained me was that others might see in her a handicap where there was none. The principal made me nervous. I felt he was waiting for us to slip up.

"Hey, Mrs. Weisz, Dana wants to sing 'Mary Had a Little Lamb'."

"You are being rude, no?" My mother bristled. In these class-room encounters our eyes didn't meet. It wasn't clear to whom we were first accountable.

My mother tried to teach me to draw, but I couldn't form a stick figure. I didn't know how to wield a paintbrush. The paint ran, smeared, made a mess. As a last resort she gave me a colour-ing book, but my crayon went over the lines.

"Look," my mother said in exasperation, pulling the crayon from my hand, "the sun is yellow, not blue. Otherwise what colour would you make the sky?"

Giving up, she bought me shoes instead, red, shiny and smooth. There wasn't a crease or a crack in them. The buckle on the strap was brassy bright, neither chipped nor scratched. They were beautiful. Against white knee socks, and worn with the navy box-pleat tunic and white cotton school blouse, they were the clarion call of child-splendour. My mother said, in Hungarian, that colour was a property of childhood. My per-fect, splendid new shoes, with the buffed black slab of heel that clicked down the school hallway—the rich, new-leather smell of them—when I looked in the mirror they leapt at the eye from under my white socks. How could something be so lovely as this red beside white?

At school the other girls wore the same T-strapped foot-wear, or loafers, but all navy or black. The boys wore brown oxfords. My red shoes were magnificent. At home I took the shoe brush and stroked them back to perfection. My shoes were undoubtedly glorious, but I knew they weren't right. Why was something not right when it was evidently best?

My friends were all girls. We sat at the front and in the middle of the class. Only the worst-behaved boys sat near us, placed under the teacher's eye. Our desks were ranged in five rows, six and seven seats deep. They were solid wood with rounded edges, smooth from the rub of books and hands, and scored by the lead of wayward pencils. We didn't use the inkwell for what it was intended. Our pens had narrow, see-through cartridges that were punctured when the casing was screwed onto the nib. Cartridges were supposed to be neater than ink bottles, but ink sometimes squirted onto the fresh white page if we weren't careful. Some girls put their recess apples into the inkwell. The boys fiddled with crumpled-up paper they stuffed down the hole and stabbed with their pencils. When the teacher left the room they stretched their arms through the desk drawer underneath and popped the wads of paper up through the holes. We pitied them.

My girlfriends were Carol, Gail, Mary, Kathy and Frances. Their last names were Dunn, Connelly, McGuire, Jones, Conway. A girl in the other grade three class was called Katzakis.

"Never heard of 'Dana'," they said when I joined the class.

They'd never heard of Hungary, either, but I pointed it out on a map.

Our teacher was a small woman who was what we called Oriental because none of us could tell the difference between Chinese and Japanese and we didn't know there are any other kinds. We could tell the ages of most of the teachers. The young ones wore their long hair piled high on their heads; the older ones wore their hair short and crimped and had thicker waists and legs. We couldn't gauge the vintage of our teacher because she looked different, but her name tipped us off; she was a "Miss."

School was the place I could show I was best. The right answers were easy. "Where did Sally take Spot? Who went to the store with Dick? Where did Jane put the eraser?" Spelling every night for homework—use these words in sentences: correct, courtesy, gallant, reward.

Some kids didn't seem to know the obvious. How could Ronnie Everett not remember that Sally took Spot to the park?

We had just finished reading about it. There was a picture of Sally kneeling beside her dog to unclasp his leash. We knew it was Sally by her blonde curly bob. Jane was taller, with brown, page-boyed hair. Ronnie Everett stood up to answer but swayed sheepishly. We spent a lot of time in class waiting for Ronnie to remember.

My mother's staffroom gossip was a door to the world of adults. I knew the new kindergarten teacher hired to assist my mother wasn't in favour. She wasn't pretty, but that couldn't be helped, said my mother. The new teacher coughed nervously whenever the principal spoke to her. My mother said the new teacher only looked awkward; she was more capable than he thought, but Gibbs would find a way to get rid of her at the end of the year. It was a shame, said my mother. The new teacher had a bad boyfriend who also made her unhappy. It wasn't easy being plain. When I went into the kindergarten to meet my mother after school, I saw the new teacher zipping the jackets of thirty little kids lined up in hats and boots. I felt a secret power knowing what was in store for her.

I knew also that Miss Osborne was getting married in the spring, but I wasn't allowed to divulge this because of Mr. Gibbs. Mr. Gibbs liked to share jokes with Miss Osborne while she stood at her classroom door watching the grade twos file in from recess. It was hard to keep my mouth shut. Miss Osborne was popular in the schoolyard too. Sometimes she was an ender for our jump ropes. In the winter, an entourage of little girls circled around her as she perambulated the schoolyard. My information was valuable currency, but I had nowhere to spend it. "If you dare breathe a word!" my mother threatened.

My mother was afraid of a number of things. She was afraid someone would complain that her language was not good enough for the job. She was afraid Mr. Gibbs would find out from a secondary source what her opinion was of him, and it would cost her dearly. She was afraid of appearing too different from the other parents, and thus being considered unfit to teach their children. At home we were admonished not to raise our voices—not against each other, but lest the neighbours overheard. What might they think—that we were uncivilized? She was afraid, in this new world, of losing what she had gained. Although I had never done so, I worried that might inadvertently shame her, tarnish her reputation and jeopardize our safety. Sometimes, in exciting exchanges between friends, I felt welling up some piece of juicy staffroom gossip. It bubbled. I actually felt it in the flow of saliva in my mouth, and the quickened pulse of my chest. I had something very compelling to say. It was physical, this desire to disclose and entertain. I was afraid one day I would let slip the forbidden.

My friend Frances tugged her striped stocking cap lower on her forehead. The wind whipped snow into our faces. We twirled around to cheat its lash. "Miss Taylor has a coat like Mrs. Atkinson." She sniffed from the cold.

"No she doesn't," argued precise Carol. "Miss Taylor's coat is grey; Mrs. Atkinson's is white."

"So, they're still the same coat."

"Mrs. Atkinson went to Bermuda at Christmas with her sister," Kathy contributed, "and they went snorkelling underwater."

"Who says?"

"She did. She told her class, and my sister Wendy has her."

"So," said Mary, "I've seen Mrs. Atkinson's sister in the parking lot. You wouldn't think she's her sister. She looks so pretty."

I swerved to put the wind at my back, and the pom-pom at the end of my windsock of a hat batted me in the mouth. As I walked backwards facing my friends my heart raced expectantly. What I knew about Mrs. Atkinson's sister would trump any parking lot sighting. My mother had said Mrs. Atkinson took her sister to Bermuda to help her feel better after she'd lost her baby. *Lost her baby!* No, my mother said, not that kind of lost, the baby wasn't real yet.

My wind-smacked cheeks didn't show the flush I knew was on them. I swallowed hard to contain my information but my voice jumped ahead of me.

"Why would Mrs. Atkinson go to Bermuda with a sister? That's weird," I challenged the panel marching me back.

Kathy shrugged. "Sisters do stuff together."

"Yeah, but what if they have husbands?" said Carol.

I thought my heart would burst, I was that close to telling. The temptation was unbearable. I swung around so I was walking abreast of my friends. Snow pelted my eyelids. "Mrs. Atkinson's sister is a Miss. She's Miss Carlisle."

I could feel sweat under my acrylic hat brim despite the windy wet. My heart slowed in relief. There, I'd said it. I'd managed to say it without crossing the line.

I knew the limits of what I was allowed. I was allowed to enter the kindergarten at the end of the day if I wanted to. This meant I might finger the toys as long as I didn't rearrange them. I might chat with the other teacher, or draw on the blackboard behind my mother's chair. These were privileges, I knew, for having a mother in the school. But I couldn't count on her to bail me out of a predicament. She'd made that clear. I had to watch my step just like the rest.

I watched myself a lot. In the mirror, I saw the perfect red leather that housed each of my careful steps. I had matched it with a red sweater that had round plastic buttons. The collar of my white blouse sat overtop. Watching what I said was as carefully pieced together. Daily I honed my self-censor, balancing between what I wanted to say and what I could not.

Mr. Gibbs was one of the few men in the school. He was big, handsome, with short thick hair of no colour. His heavy moustache matched. Way up from his height we felt the sting of his blue eyes always watchful and suspicious, as though just because we were kids we were bound to be up to something. He barked his instructions. When he smiled we thought of the slick-haired villain in a silent movie, tying the heroine to the track. My mother said, how this man had come to run a school for little children was beyond her. He had been a sergeant in the army once upon a time. I was sensitive to once-upon-a-times and had no trouble grasping metamorphosis. The other men were Mr. Wainright, the gym teacher, and Mr. James, who unaccountably taught grade four. Mr. Burgess headed up the grade sevens because they were the oldest and needed a firm hand. Otherwise there was only Mr. Beaudry, the custodian. There were three classes at each grade except kindergarten, making Mr. Gibbs's staff of women around twenty.

We were used to women. Men were a shadowy presence. We met our friends' fathers on weekends as they sat behind the wheel of a car to drop us off at Brownies or swimming. We weren't expected to speak to them while we giggled with our friends in the back seat. My piano teacher was Mr. Hansen. He had a quiet voice and a soft accent my mother said was Dutch. Mr. Hansen came to our house. He smelled of shaving cream and wore rumpled shiny grey suits. He leaned over me from behind and covered my hands on the keys to show me what I was doing wrong. Mr. Hansen's touch was as neutral as water.

I tensed at the sound of Mr. Gibbs's voice heartily booming down the corridor as he shook hands with the consultant. Something about the way he filled his sandy-shaded lightweight suits made me nervous, and so did the dark pipe clenched inside strong teeth. He was the only one in the school who smoked outside the staffroom. If you were sent at lunchtime to take a note to the teachers' lounge, the cigarette haze burned your eyes. My mother walked home for her lunch because she couldn't stand the smoke, but she said, too, that watching Mr. Gibbs flirt with the young teachers put her off her food. He pestered them but they felt obliged to laugh and smile.

Sometimes a teacher was a Miss although she looked like a Mrs. This was uncommon. Mrs. Dunbar, the secretary, had no husband because he was dead. Mrs. Grace, the librarian, was older too and came to staff parties unaccompanied. But to be a Miss with lines on her face, there was only Miss Armstrong like that, and Mr. Gibbs disliked her. He dropped in on her classes after he had lurked around until he heard the highest level of noise. Then he barged in and, in the din of desks and chairs being pushed back abruptly, he roared, "This class can be heard *all the way down the hall!*" Sure, said my mother, you mean heard from right behind the door. She thought Miss

Armstrong was a good teacher and hoped she'd still be around when I reached grade five.

I wasn't sure why Mr. Gibbs didn't like Miss Armstrong, but it had something to do with her being a Miss and having thick ankles and wearing pleated tartan the colour of dried blood. My mother said you needed to be slim to wear pleats. I found Miss Armstrong somewhat formidable and didn't share my mother's enthusiasm for having her as my teacher, but I doubted Mr. Gibbs objected to her on account of us children.

My mother and Mr. Gibbs had an unsteady relationship. No one was totally secure with him, but my mother felt reasonably confident. She had supporters at the school board. She managed to restrain the multiplying, squirming bodies whose little bottoms polished more of the kindergarten floor each September. She was married-untouchable, and seasoned enough to elude the bloom of his interest. But, unlike Mrs. Chandler, for instance, or Mrs. Butler, or Mrs. Harrington, who were all middle-aged and Anglo, my mother was an immigrant, and this sometimes shifted her ground.

"Mrs. Weisz." He pronounced our name as Wise. Others on staff had learned a decent rendition that sounded like the word "Vice," but he avoided it. "Wise" was more ironic. "Mrs. Wise," he smirkingly inflected, "I believe the correct usage is 'tamper.' We say, 'Don't tamper with the light switch,' not 'Don't temper with it.' It is I who have a temper." At which cue my mother's colleagues were expected to join in with snickers. I was amazed that my mother risked expanding her vocabulary when these pitfalls were certain. But she was, said Mrs. Chandler sympathetically, a tough cookie. "You're a tough cookie, Mrs. Weisz, you can take it, don't worry." Tough cookie though she may have been, my mother burned with indignation.

At home one afternoon the pots were clanged and banged to the stovetop. There were vicious expletives against cupboard doors that thwarted her, a garbage can that didn't shut.

"It's up to me, always me," she vented in Hungarian. "I have to put the garbage out too—only I see that it's stinking, over-flowing. I have to take care of everything."

It was prudent to lie low. No one else was at home. My father and sister would arrive in time for dinner. There were only me and the garbage can to catch the brunt of her wrath. Something must have happened with a parent, maybe, and the principal. Perhaps he hadn't backed her up as she'd expected. After supper I overheard her in the bedroom with my father.

"He has gone too far now. This is unbearable. In my classroom. Anyone could walk in and see them. What if a parent? Just me this time. But next time who? One of the children? He won't let me forget this!"

My mother was afraid of what she had seen. What she had witnessed was dangerous knowledge.

"To me. On purpose. No coincidence. A slap to me in the face."

I wanted to go in to her. I wanted to assure her that we were safe here. Nothing could happen. This was a free world, a new world. Here it was safe to be Jewish, to have an accent, and to speak your mind. That's what it said in the law. My sister at the university told me these things. But my mother would have shaken me off. She mistrusted all authorities.

I was more afraid of my mother's anguish than of any threat from Mr. Gibbs. It brought us too close to what she had escaped. Suddenly the past was beside us, brushing us with terror. It was after dinner, but I felt starved. My hunger was gnawing and frightful. Her fear crazed me.

There was often noise in our family. We didn't always realize why. A trap door would trigger open, the atmosphere become charged. We yelled at each other a lot before it was over.

I seemed to be shouting now. "There are no more socks! I have no socks for tomorrow! Brown socks! Who needs brown socks? I can't wear brown socks with my tunic!"

I was infuriated by her fear, so misplaced. Was she blind? Was she stupid? There were no Nazis here, just a blustering principal. How could she not know this? I believed it like a faith: the badness was over. It lay behind us with the past.

The next day in the corridor I regarded Mr. Gibbs with contempt. He left his trace of pipe odour behind him in the halls to remind us of his presence. He filled his pressed suits tightly to show off his strength. He flashed his teeth in his smile, framed each request as an order. He was the first man I had met who presented his maleness before his intellect. There was something pathetic in this, like Billy Tait the class bully, a meanness that begged to be punished.

My mother saw in the petty tyrant an evil it was her duty to suppress. We heard at supper one evening how she had gone in to see the principal, closing the door behind her.

"Mr. Gibbs," she began. She looked at him across his desk. She said that because he was sitting they could see eye to eye. "Mr. Gibbs," she repeated, "you are the principal. You are in charge. This is a school, Mr. Gibbs. I have only a classroom, but it is my classroom. My classroom, Mr. Gibbs. You are the principal. You have an *office*. Next time, Mr. Gibbs, use your office."

I imagined her turning on her flats, daring to expose her back.

My mother had mustered all her resources for this sally, leaving her shaken. When I arrived home after school, she was already in the La-Z-Boy with a compress on her forehead. She didn't feel she had fought back, although that was how it struck me. She didn't feel powerful. For my mother, each day, each tussle was a struggle of equal bearing to keep herself upright.

Mr. Gibbs didn't live in our suburb, but somewhere in the city. It was a shock, therefore, to see him on the weekend, in one of those tweed caps that snapped together in the front. I was swinging a drawstring bag that held my ballet slippers. I loved this bag. It was encrusted with clear, multicoloured beads. As I swung it open-armed, the beads caught the light.

The recent snow had frozen over, making the sidewalks treacherous for grown-ups. We children loved it. You could shave five minutes off your walk-home time if you slid. Slide over two sidewalk squares. Running start, slide over three sidewalk squares. Swing your bag, running start, *gli-s-s-ade*—I liked the French word for it better. It was like ballet.

Mr. Gibbs had just closed the door of a honey brick duplex and was descending its stairs carefully, holding onto the black railing. He reached the last step before I registered who he was. A reflex, I felt as though I'd done something wrong.

No running in the halls!

And where do you think you're going?

I wanted to turn around and pretend I hadn't seen him, but it was Saturday, I remembered. It was Saturday, I was allowed where I pleased. What was *he* doing here? He was the one out of place. This wasn't fair, we had a right to our free days, our school-less days, our Mr. Gibbs-not-hanging-over-our-heads days. He caught sight of me as he glanced up from the bottom step. My bag, still swinging from the last slide, bounced ice-light from its surface like a toy mace. I stood my ground while he advanced.

"Hello, Mr. Gibbs."

He hesitated briefly, then touched the brim of his hat. "Dana. You're looking jolly."

Jolly?!

We sized each other up. He was wearing a short leather coat belted at the waist. It made him look thick in the middle.

"Where're you off to then?" he asked.

And a lizard sprang unbidden from my mouth, its forked tongue vibrating. "None of your business!"

Aghast, I turned rigid with fear, rooted to the spot. I felt I'd turned into one of those sooty, icy stands of snow that lined the street all winter.

"I beg your pardon?" he questioned, doubting his ears.

But the lizard darted a second time. My tongue had turned reptilian and volatile. "Where do you think *you're* going? Kissing Miss Casey again?"

The ice broke the spell by tripping me forward. Run, run, run. My shoebag swung in giant arcs as I raced, stumbled and slid. A joyous crash of light-striking colour radiated around me. Breathless, sobbing, hysterically jubilant, this time I'd done it.

Daily the waited summons to the office failed to materialize. Whenever there was a knock at the classroom door and I heard my teacher murmur with someone in the hall, my stomach clenched. This was it. I would be expected to present myself with my mother—yes, my mother, because I had incriminated her even more than myself. We would be called for sentencing.

Despite my sense of doom, I felt unrepentant. The thought of my offence buoyed me. The jolt of blue under Mr. Gibbs's arching brows. My wild skidding dance along the runway of our street.

It was my mother I feared. Her rage was electric. Once trapped in its current you fried. She woke the next morning still charged. No, I'd no wish to trip the switch on my mother, but expected she'd find out anyway.

The week went by without a call to the office. I avoided Mr. Gibbs. This wasn't hard since his loud voice and strong cologne proclaimed his approach. I steered clear of him.

As winter warmed into the first crystal slushes of spring, I started to feel easier. Mr. Gibbs had sought no revenge. It appeared he no more wished to draw attention to our encounter than I did. I had done him a favour perhaps, by supplying my own reason to keep quiet.

I emerged from hiding, took to meeting my mother in the kindergarten after school. He was often in front of the office. "Hello, Mr. Gibbs," I said boldly, trying to hold his eye. I acted as though nothing had happened, as if I knew nothing about him I shouldn't. I let him know there was nothing to conceal. At first he shifted his weight uneasily, remembering a task elsewhere. But my performance was so convincing he finally relaxed. Eventually he could tolerate my standing quietly by my mother's side as they discussed school matters. I thought he might actually come to question I had ever known anything I shouldn't, decide that my outburst had been a wild fabrication by an imaginative child that had chanced to land on target.

Spring in the suburb was for children. The pavement dried quickly and you could bring out the bikes when the first strong sunny afternoon made pools of the yards. Jump ropes were pulled from the bottom of toy chests. Ball-o-bats appeared instantly on store shelves, and we doffed our coats at lunchtime to walk back to school in pullovers, under the wide blue sky. Snow melted off driveways that sloped towards the street. After school we tied a rope end to the garage door handle and skipped our first jumps of the season. The world in a suburban spring was spacious and full of promise.

The town smelled like running water. Melting snow cascaded in the gutters. We heard it spill down the sewers. The drug-store displayed spring candy: sponges like honeycomb that welded to our teeth, wax lips we sucked for their red sap then chewed into candle wax we spit into the street, candy neck-laces of pastel O's we wore around our bare necks and mouthed the whole afternoon. We showed off, wearing Brownie uniforms for all the world to admire. The town matched us in age, grew with us, drew from us its inspiration. The six doors on my family's duplex were each a different primary colour. The Royal Bank in the shopping centre repainted its sedate interior a bright orange. The town was ours. Our spinning bicycle wheels possessed its streets, skimmed through puddles and left snake-like trails.

My mother said she noticed a change in the way Mr. Gibbs talked to her. He seemed to have lost his appetite for baiting. Scanning the kindergarten one day, its raucous display of colour and the children on the floor calmly playing, he conceded, "I don't know how you do it, Mrs. Weisz. We couldn't get along without you."

"He said 'Vice.' He pronounced it properly!" she observed with mixed pleasure, piqued with herself to have been caught off guard.

Eichmann's

Monogram

Mummy said not to be silly. She happened to know that the teacher I'd be getting at the new school was the best of the grade two teachers. The teacher was good, and one grade two class was the same as another. I'd have no problem switching. She couldn't understand what the difficulty was anyway. We'd be in our new house. A brand-new house—ours—and finally I'd have my own bedroom. "Really, Dana," she summed up, "I have no time for your nonsense."

I had no argument with the new house. A new house was wonderful, but why couldn't I start the new school in September, like her, instead of waiting a month until we moved in? By then everyone in the class would know each other, and I'd be the only one left out.

Mummy was pleased to have gotten a job teaching in the new neighbourhood's school. We'd be in the same school and she'd be able to watch out for me and give me lunch at home. I was smart enough to appreciate a practical situation.

I was also starting to realize that if I weren't always such an obliging child, she wouldn't keep moving me around at her convenience. Counting the nursery school I went to when we first arrived in Canada, the new school in Ville d'Anjou would be my third. And one grade two class wasn't the same as another. I dreaded having to be a newcomer again.

This move in October unnerved me. Through spring and summer my parents had spoken of little else. The purchase, the decision, where Mummy would work. Plans and speculations were nothing new, but these had been interspersed with references to a trial in Israel.

Should they go, shouldn't they?

Go where? What for?

It would cost too much, and what with buying the house, they needed every penny. Others would testify.

By the hundreds. By now the world knew plenty.

Their stories wouldn't be missed. There was evidence enough to hang him a million times.

"A million times," erupted Mummy, higher-pitched. "A million times would be too few. He destroyed more than a million. What about the rest? He destroyed me as well!" By now she was loud enough for the neighbours to hear.

"Sári, enough," Apu had interrupted, "we're not going. Be reasonable. Why do we need to go there? It might not be safe. Think of the children, if something happened to us."

They were still talking about Eichmann. *Eichmann.* The name that drew silences but was suddenly always in the air. Eichmann caged for his own *protection.* Why shouldn't they testify? Apu alone claimed eighty dead. And Mummy. Mummy had survived Auschwitz. They *should* go. They had plenty to tell.

"No," Apu finished, "I will not see that face."

I filled with dread over the coming move. I pictured the strange children turning to stare at me as I was introduced to the class. I thought of having no one to play with at recess, and remembered the loneliness of the last schoolyard where I had been left off early each morning when Mummy went to work. Waiting in the winter cold, the empty schoolgrounds spread out before me. Hoping for another child to turn up. Thinking maybe

I wasn't early. Maybe I was late, so late everyone else was already inside and I had missed everything important.

I remembered the old stories. Not the good, daytime ones about the former Perfect World, but the nightmares of terror and loss I had overheard my parents recount at night. I remembered the helplessness of adults who couldn't stop the badness from taking place. The adults powerless as children and unable to protect them. And now he was trapped like an animal in a cage, this *Eichmann*, this *person*, this *old man*. I couldn't stand hearing Apu object to going to Israel. It was intolerable that he said they should do nothing. Hadn't they already done nothing? All of them. The good, kind grandfather, and the pious, loving grandmother, and the as-it-turned-out not-so-clever sons—Apu and his brothers—university laureates, but who cared, if in the end they were masters of nothing, certainly not their fates.

The teacher in the new class was very tall and thin with her hair piled high. She spoke in the clipped and authoritative tones of the British. Pinning a picture over the blackboard, she unfurled a yellow duckling swimming on a blue pond beside a red barn.

"Boys and girls, for this week's composition I want you to write a story about what you see in this picture."

Composition. My blood froze. What was that? *Composition,* something complicated and technical, far beyond my powers. *This week's! A composition each week!* This grade two certainly wasn't the same as the other.

I started to cry. The English lady bent over me, and I smelled the false powdery sweetness of her perfume. She patted my shoulder. "That's all right, Dana. Your composition can be about yourself."

Composition—that word again! I cried all morning. I cried when a girl was assigned to be my partner to go out to the recess yard. And I cried at lunch even though Mummy told me I'd be a laughingstock if I kept this up.

I cried daily in that class for the first two weeks, embarrassing my mother in front of her new principal and colleagues. Did I want them to think her child was a "problem"?

"Really, Dana, you know you could write down a few words if you tried."

Not that I cried all the time. I jumped rope in the recess yard, and walked one day after school to the home of a class-mate to play. I did my arithmetic, and felt pleased to be one of the last ones out in an all-class spelling bee. But whenever the English lady came up beside me to say, "Dana, won't you just write a word or two about yourself?" I started to cry.

I didn't know why, exactly. The thought of writing anything except practice letters and spelling words was overwhelming and beyond me. It felt so good to give in and know it was too much. It was all too much, what they expected of me. It was more than I was capable of. And it felt good, so good, to show it. I would not write for this British person despite her smile and interesting hair piled in a beehive. I would perform no more tricks.

"What do you make me look like?" snapped my mother. "Do you want them to think I can't raise my own child properly?"

I listened to the other children read aloud their stories about ducklings. I watched as a new picture got clipped to the black-board a week later. This one showed a family, a boy, a girl, a mother and father, somewhere among strange structures—a huge wheel with people on it, and an elaborate giant slide thing that went up and down in waves. The children in the picture held sticks with something pink and fuzzy that looked like the top of my teacher's hairdo. She rested her hands on my shoulders. "Won't you write something, Dana, about yourself?"

After two weeks I relented, stopped snivelling and wrote my first composition. The teacher let me take it home. Mummy laughed, showing it to Apu and my sister Lillian.

"All this bawling over nothing. Look here," she said.

I had written in pencil pressed so hard into the paper it had broken through in places: **I was born in Hungry. My sister was born in Hungry. My mother was born in Hungry. My father was born in Hungry.**

"So," said Mummy, laughing, "this was the big news?"

By December 1961, we were settled in. The new living-room suite was delivered and the old secondhand set that had been bought for the apartment was relegated to the basement TV room. By December I had made new friends, joined Brownies, taken up the recorder; I hung on my teacher's every word as on a prophet's. In December, even without Mummy and Apu's testimonies, Eichmann's sentence was passed.

Apu started digging that spring. In the fall he had managed only to tame the lawn. It had grown wild and he couldn't pass the mower through it. First he had to bend over double to cut out big swaths with pruning shears that looked like a giant's nail scissors. Then he used the mower, its rotary blades clogging with green muck. He tugged the mower back, pushed forward, pulled back, pushed ahead. He inched his way over the back yard until we had something to walk on instead of through.

But in spring his real gardening began. As soon as the ground had thawed enough and while it was still soggy and pliant, he started to dig holes. He dug so many, in the evenings as the days grew longer, and on weekends, that I thought he'd gotten fed up with the lawn and wanted to do away with it altogether. Down the right-hand border beside the fence, he dug six holes equidistant from each other. In these would go the flowering shrubs: forsythia, honeysuckle, spiraea, hydrangea, lilac and snowball. Along the left-hand border that was open to the other neighbour he cut a deep ridge for a hedge. Across the top of the garden he dug pits for trees: crabapple, hawthorne, apple and pear. Last, he dug the one in the middle of the yard for the tree that was supposed to produce shade for Mummy's webbed lawn chair.

I laughed at the puny thing he put in the centre of the big yard. Mummy had better drape a scarf over her face for her summer siestas. It would take quite a while for those twigs to give shade. But he wasn't finished. Apu dug a wide flower bed around the skinny sapling. Then, on his hands and knees, he put in the plantings: red salvia closest to the measly trunk,

yellow marigolds in the middle, and white alyssum for the edge.
With his hands in the earth, and his gardening hat on his bald-
ing pate, Apu said Kaddish for the dead.

He chanted the Hebrew words that I recognized from the Yom
Kippur service when the house was veiled in mourning, curtains
drawn and memorial candles aflicker. Lili and I were barred from
this ritual, not because Mummy and Apu required privacy but
so we wouldn't be branded by their grief. But out here in the
garden in spring, under the clear sky, Apu openly spoke the
words for the dead, not afraid that I or the neighbours would
overhear. I wondered if all this digging and praying meant he
was finally burying them. When he stood, eventually, to survey
his work around the weeping willow, he wiped his hands on his
trousers and pulled me close. He held me in silence, staring with
wet eyes at the little tree.

"Too bad, Danuska," he said in the Hungarian he always
spoke at home, "too bad that on the last day the Lord chose
to rest."

Too bad. The Lord took a nap, and the serpent spoiled His
garden. Seventeen years had passed since the Hungarian depor-
tations. The Lord had taken His time to awake. On the last
day in May in the first spring of our new life, Eichmann was
hanged.

Along crescent streets muffled in snow, zipper-hooded adven-
turers emerged to plod past the split levels whose rooflines had
oddly descended. Overnight the snow had risen, obliterating
the primary hues of doorways, and filling the undeveloped fields
with a crystalline blankness that felt like the start of the world.
Nylon snowsuits crackled as our buckled boots broke trails to
the park that joined our crescents. Children were first to venture out into that white sea that frothed over our boot tops.
Station wagons stayed landlocked in carports. Businesses, like
adults, stalled, opened late. Shovels came out after we were
already in our seats, socks damp inside buffed leather. Puddles
formed in lockers. By lunchtime we could spring home on
firm treads left by sidewalk plows, and crunch up the walks

shovelled clear by fathers before they'd left for work. But in the opening bars of those winter preludes we sounded the first notes. We children of morning in the new world. A world pure in its erasure of woods and pasture, where even the rutted earth that filled in the spring with pools that spawned tadpoles was a transitional ecosystem, promising streets that were newer yet than those bordered by saplings that matched us in height; streets as obliquely connecting, navigable only by automobile and bicycle and humming happily with the mechanical whirs of an emerging world.

I had fallen in love with the newness of Ville d'Anjou. I loved the shape of the houses, spare and angular. I loved their bright colours. I loved the playground and its futuristic apparatus. The painted bars of the rocket ship that, last summer, I was still afraid to climb to the top. The clean sand. The amoeba-shaped wading pool painted aqua like the sky. I adopted this landscape, having come from a world that history had disfavoured. Like a false start, it shouldn't have happened. My place now was among the split levels, bungalows and duplexes of Ville d'Anjou—a world without war or want or fear—on the eastern edge of Montreal. The last inhabitable outpost before the island's desert stretch of refineries. A glimpse of the future sliced from farmers' fields and nestled like a spare-edged brilliant inside a baroque setting. The east end's characteristically dark brick façades were heavily curtained with evergreens. Spiral, two-storey staircases, curling with black grillwork, twined up the fronts of prewar walk-ups. We had had to negotiate those dark streets like a journey through the past before breathing a lighter ether once we turned north from Sherbrooke Street and climbed—not uphill, there was no grade though I could feel myself lift—into a largesse of land and air, yes, more air; the homes hardly impinged on the sky. I exhaled once we reached Chenier Street after the march of duplexes from Sherbrooke. On Chenier the bungalows began, and the ranch-styles low and sprawling.

In those tidy, self-contained domiciles, children knelt on wall-to-wall carpeting, watching electric trains rock around a track.

Little girls hauled about blonde-haired dolls as tall as themselves, pulling a ring on the neck to hear words in English.
Their dinners, absurdly premature, were at four in the afternoon, when my mother was lying exhausted, feet up in the
La-Z-Boy. Their bedtimes were punishingly early when in our
house we were still eating—well—not from a box. I didn't envy
them. But there was something certain in the heavy hang of a
thick and perfect ringlet suspended from a plaid ribbon. A location in time and place. A privilege in knowing trends, and a
luxury in caring about them. I hankered for the sureness of these
gestures. Inside picture windows young-looking mothers stayed
home and dangled legs beside telephone tables. I loved this
vision of ease and belonging. Living rooms were off limits when
you stepped in after school. A glimpse of perfect composure like
an unblemished face. My family's duplex was new, but branded
with economic expedience, a paying tenant and the proximi-
ties of shared walls. It made me feel set apart, as did my older
parents, and working mother, and empty garage.

On winter mornings my father was long gone on his trek by
public transport to Bernstein's downtown office. Our front walk
was a crisp scar in the white expanse that had filled overnight,
and the sidewalk in front a smooth swath to the neighbour's
invisible border. He wouldn't let my mother risk climbing over
snowbanks to the street where, he hoped, at least a car or two
would have left a track for her to walk in, for my mother, like
me, had to make it in time for the schoolyard bell. She'd leave
before me, giving herself extra minutes because the snowfall
would slow her down, to be ready to greet her class at the
kindergarten entrance. I noticed her pointy-toed boot prints and
made my blunt-nosed marks beside them.

Dire threats of penicillin injections had impressed me with
the need to dress properly for the cold: not only hat but scarf,
not just jacket but also sweater. Two pairs of mittens, for one
was bound to get wet. Sometimes, during her exams, my sister
would be home to lock the door behind me. More often she
left early with my father for her classes at Mountview High. I
locked the door with the key that hung like a charm under my

cotton school blouse, and went out with the other children, into the snow.

My over-swaddled burliness made each step an extra effort as I waded through the wet snow on Boulevard de la Loire. Rounding the corner onto Croissy Circle, I took in a sudden, frigid draft of air. Immediately, it was not *my* hand that I felt burrowed in the quilted lining of a nylon pocket; it was my hand grasped inside someone's larger woollen mitten. The past came on me like that. In a breath. An uncomfortable intrusion like the intake of cold air. I was working my way through the deep snow behind the Budapest tenement, my sister's hand firmly clasping mine and tugging me up the white hill looming largely ahead. My sister the school-going age I was now. My sister big to my small. Our woollen jackets heavy with wet snow. The prickly leggings bunched between our legs rubbing thickly together. My panting breath behind the scarf a wet, thready steam forming an icy crust that grazed my nostrils. Trudging up, up, plodding sweatily in the cold. I followed my sister anywhere. Going up. Hurtling down. I assumed unquestioningly some good reason for our labour in that whiteness.

The memory was alive, vivid and concurrent. I felt it. In Ville d'Anjou, on the fifteen-minute walk to school through snow up to my kneecaps, hot with effort under my nylon and zippers, snot crystallizing on the scarf over my mouth, and snow stinging, not yet wet, as it bit over my boot tops, I'd slide back. Not through pictures, or snapshots, or narrative, but through a physical sensation of being in different worlds at once.

That year I learned how to iron on my father's monogrammed handkerchiefs. These, already worn and, according to my mother, needlessly time-consuming in Canada where there was no lack of paper, would be suitable for practice. I had the time, and if I scorched or stained them, my forbearing father wouldn't complain.

The pointlessness of these handkerchiefs annoyed me. Just rags made for soiling, it seemed stupid to have to iron them. They were out of place in the new sunlit suburban kitchen, but then so was my father, old-world in his manners and values, and plain old compared to the fathers of my friends. No one who saw my father in the modern kitchen, dishcloth in hand, could guess he had been a person of consequence in another time in his life, someone who had run a large agricultural concern, and belonged to a dynasty that had dominated its community. My father was a mild, past-middle-aged immigrant who took three buses into the city each morning to his book-keeping job at a rag-trade wholesaler's. He shrank from deal-ings with French-Canadian tradesmen who he sensed despised his mechanical helplessness as well as his linguistic impediment. He felt scorned because he knew nothing about hammers or water pipes or electrical outlets, when in the old days labour-ers had done those tasks on his family's estate. It was hard for me to reconcile my father in Canada with the image of the world he had come from and conjured. That world had shrunk to the proportions of his handkerchiefs.

Grudgingly I took up the chore of ironing them. At first I resented the time it stole from Brownie badges and ballet. I would shake open the handkerchiefs roughly and hold the iron above them like a threat. But I couldn't resist first fingering the scroll of my father's raised initials, reversed in the Hungarian practice of surname first. I traced the letters, bemused, pitying. Imagine a world so guileless it bothered to initial linens believ-ing they would last a lifetime, just like it assumed a life unfolds in one place.

I grew protective, spread the cotton flat on the ironing board with my open palms and followed the pencil-thin borders that framed grey checks and solid manly hues. An uncompromising light flooded through the wall-high window behind me and passed through each thread, showing how the weave had pulled open and thinned. I began to handle the handkerchiefs like artifacts. I stroked the worn fabric, feeling how tenuous was my connection to that other time, that other place of which remained only these threadbare remnants. I brought the iron down with care, anticipating the hiss as heat hit damp cloth, the steam of this union producing soft layers I folded precisely, matching up the edges.

I considered myself light years from the world of my father's old photographs and anecdotes. Ville d'Anjou was the future. We had inherited nothing here. It was all brand-new, the trees twiglike and the gardens bare. The bright paint on sharp-sloped roofs was a first application. The scent of sawdust seeped from the framework in the houses. I felt I had sprung fully formed into this landscape. I had been dreamed into a world without war or want, and I started at this point, like the bushes and trees my father planted our first spring in the new house. Mummy and Apu had once occupied a terrain blasted by uncertainty, loss and terror. My world was new. My life, lucky child of fortune born after the Holocaust, had slid open like the ironing board onto a clean slate of blue and white linoleum tile.